WINDS OF L'ACADIE

Winds of L'Acadie

Lois Donovan

RONSDALE PRESS

WINDS OF L'ACADIE
Copyright © 2007 Lois Donovan
Third Printing March 2011

RONSDALE PRESS
3350 West 21st Avenue, Vancouver, B.C., Canada V6S 1G7
www.ronsdalepress.com

Typesetting: Julie Cochrane, in Minion 12 pt on 16
Front Cover Art: Ljuba Levstek
Cover Design: Julie Cochrane
Paper: Ancient Forest Friendly Rolland "Enviro" — 100% post-consumer
    waste, totally chlorine-free and acid-free

Ronsdale Press wishes to thank the Canada Council for the Arts, the Government of Canada through the Book Publishing Industry Development Program (BPIDP), and the Province of British Columbia through the British Columbia Arts Council for their support of its publishing program.

Library and Archives Canada Cataloguing in Publication

Donovan, Lois, 1955–
    Winds of l'Acadie / Lois Donovan.

    ISBN-13: 978-1-55380-047-7
    ISBN-10: 1-55380-047-8

    1. Acadians — Expulsion, 1755 — Juvenile fiction. I. Title.

PS8607.O68W56 2007   jC813'.6   C2007-900105-X

At Ronsdale Press we are committed to protecting the environment. To this end we are working with Markets Initiative (www.oldgrowthfree.com) and printers to phase out our use of paper produced from ancient forests. This book is one step towards that goal.

Printed in Canada by Marquis Printing, Quebec

*To Jared, who is waiting
for the movie to come out.
To Grace, who is still
reading Brown Bear.
To Patrick, for always
believing in me.
Thank you for your loving
support, encouragement
and inspiration.*

ACKNOWLEDGEMENTS

I would like to thank Ronald Hatch at Ronsdale Press for his endless patience and encouragement throughout the revision process. Thanks are also due to the many people who provided helpful feedback and support as the novel evolved. Jenny Thiessen faithfully read and gave honest feedback throughout the original writing of the novel. Mr. Donovan's Grade Six class at Sir James Lougheed listened to the entire first draft with encouraging enthusiasm. Anna Mae Siegel read and reread the manuscript, providing tips and useful insights as well as proofreading for errors. Her gift of an authentic quill box inspired its role as a time-travel device. Cathy Beveridge's expertise in the writing/publishing process was much appreciated.

I would also like to thank Steve Relton, a Mi'kmaq artist in Nova Scotia, who spent considerable time explaining the making of a quill box in the traditional Mi'kmaq way. The staff members at Saint Anne's University in Nova Scotia, the Public Archives of Nova Scotia and Wolfville Tourism, and the University of Moncton were all extremely friendly and helpful in providing information and answering any questions. Lastly, a special thanks to Victor Tétrault for answering questions regarding the Grande-Pré National Historic Site of Canada.

Every attempt has been made to preserve the historical accuracy surrounding the events of the deportation of the Acadians. Colonel Winslow and Governor Lawrence are historical figures. The characters of the story, however, are fictional.

Chapter 1

"I imagine you'll find our little town pretty dull after the bright lights of Toronto," drawled Sarah's grandfather, dragging out each word the way the winding road seemed determined to drag out the drive from the airport.

Dull? Dull described paint faded from the sun. An overcast day was dull. No, dull was not the word that came to mind as Sarah anticipated the long summer ahead. This promised to be the most ridiculous thing her mother had ever asked her to endure. What a waste of a summer! Most people hadn't even heard of Wolfville, Nova Scotia.

"It'll be an interesting change, I expect," Sarah replied politely, disgusted at how much like her mother she had just sounded. She leaned her head against the headrest and pretended to sleep. She didn't feel like talking right now.

As Sarah closed her eyes she could hear her mother's pleading voice.

"It's only for two months, Sarah. Imagine ocean breezes blowing through the quaint little village. What's not to like?" Her mother checked her reflection in the mirror, patting her stylish auburn hair. "The summer will be over before you know it, and then we'll go somewhere exotic for a week together. Promise." She touched up her lipstick then glanced at her watch. "Now be a dear and don't fuss so much. You know how I hate fussing. This travel series we're shooting in southern France is on an impossible schedule. You'd hate it." Sarah had felt like screaming, not that it would have made any difference.

So here she was in the middle of nowhere Nova Scotia, while her mother, the beautiful Nicole White, host and producer of *Travel with Us*, frolicked in the south of France.

The last time Sarah had been to her grandparents' place had been fourteen years ago when she was two. That summer ended in a huge fight, which her mother refused to talk about. After that they never went back. Now she expected Sarah to spend the entire summer with them. What was with that? Maybe her mother thought she needed a father figure. It was a little late now. Grandparents were for spoiling little kids.

"See that farmland over there?" Sarah's grandfather

asked, interrupting her thoughts. "All that land was marshland that the Acadians reclaimed in the sixteen hundreds. Take a close look at that grassy hill over there with the dirt road on top. That's a dyke, still intact hundreds of years later. Incredible, isn't it? All this land would have been waste marshland if the Acadians hadn't built the dykes and washed the land of the sea salt. Mighty smart for peasants, I'd say."

"The deportation of the Acadians," Sarah said more to herself than to her grandfather. "I remember that story from school." Everything went fuzzy as she took a closer look. The heat must be getting to her. The dyke was blurred like an out-of-focus photograph. Sarah blinked in an attempt to clear her vision. Then everything was crystal clear again. "That was weird," Sarah muttered under her breath.

"What did you say?" her grandfather asked. "I didn't quite hear you."

"I was just saying that the dykes are very interesting." Sarah wasn't sure what had just happened, but she didn't want her grandfather to think she was crazy.

"Interesting and very clever," her grandfather commented. "The Grand-Pré National Historic Site has an impressive Interpretive Centre that tells the Acadian history and how the dykes work," he continued. "There are people dressed up tending the gardens and cottages out back and everything. If you're interested maybe we could go tomorrow."

"Sure." Sarah caught a glimpse of a smile in her grandfather's eyes. Pete White was distinguished looking, with his closely cropped silvery white hair and prominent cheek-bones.

She looked out the window at the orchards of neatly ordered apple trees separated by brightly painted houses. Off in the distance, the deep blue of Minas Basin glittered under the midday sun. This breathtaking valley could rival anything she had seen when travelling with her mother. Sarah sighed. Lately her mother had been including her less and less, saying dumb things, like it was time that she branched out with her own friends and her own life. As if she liked being her mother's shadow. Her mother wasn't even around enough to know that she didn't have any friends. Not any close friends, at least.

"I'm going to pick up some fresh strawberries for your grandmother." The shiny blue Ford pickup came to a stop at a bustling outdoor market. "You might as well stretch yer legs a bit."

"This is as bad as rush hour on the subway," Sarah muttered as she squeezed through the throngs of people huddled over the fresh produce. A sundress would definitely have been a better choice, she thought. She pulled at the silk top that now clung to her like plastic wrap. Pausing for a moment, she shaded her eyes against the bright rays of the sun. Despite the buzz of activity under the green-striped canopy, everyone seemed happy and relaxed. Not pinched and worried-looking like in Toronto, where everyone had to be somewhere half an hour ago.

"Sarah, over here!" Her grandfather waved to her from the other side of the market. "Got some folks I want ya to meet." Every head in the market turned in her direction. Sarah felt the curious stares as she walked past. She wanted to melt into a puddle on the ground right then and there. Thankfully she didn't know anyone within a thousand miles of here. She carefully wound her way through the stands of fruits and vegetables trying not to let her new skirt touch anything. Her mother didn't think she should meet her grandparents in shorts so she had settled for this cool purple print skirt made from Thai silk that she had found at her favourite boutique.

"This pretty flower is my granddaughter, Sarah." Pete White beamed with pride. "Sarah, I'd like you to meet our next-door neighbours, Mr. and Mrs. Outhouse."

"Pardon me?" Sarah was sure she must have heard wrong. What kind of a name was Outhouse?

"You can call us Dorothy and Roger, dear," the short round woman chirped.

Still wondering about the odd name, Sarah reached out to shake hands with the couple.

"Excuse me," said a pleasant voice behind her.

Sarah turned to find herself looking into the tanned face of a rather nice-looking guy. That's when he tripped, launching a tray of Grade A mini-missiles. In her attempt to get out of the line of fire, Sarah slipped on her high-heeled sandals and landed in a slimy puddle of shells and yolks. "Oh no, my skirt is ruined." She glared at the cause of her humiliating tumble.

"Sorry about that," the youth mumbled as he rushed to grab some paper towels.

An icy glare was Sarah's only reply as she ignored the outstretched hand offering to help her. She was embarrassed beyond words and wished he'd leave her alone.

"Suit yourself." He handed her the paper towels and then walked away.

Her grandfather helped her to her feet as several of the women rushed to Sarah's rescue clucking about stain-removal remedies and oohing over the elegant silk. Sarah just wanted to get out of there. She hoped never to see any of these people again, particularly the klutz who had dropped the eggs. Just as they were about to leave, she spotted him heading towards her. She quickly looked the other way. The last thing she wanted was some lame apology.

"Sorry again about the low-flying eggs. They're usually not so out of control."

"I'm fine," Sarah replied coolly, ignoring his attempt at humour.

"I really am sorry."

Sarah turned abruptly from him and headed toward the truck.

"It was an accident, ya know," her grandfather said as they pulled out of the parking lot.

"I know." Sarah's voice was barely audible.

"You acted mighty angry back there."

She knew she should make some sort of apology for her behaviour but couldn't quite bring herself to say anything. Anyway, it wasn't as though it was her fault the guy dropped the eggs. What a great start to the summer!

꧁

Luke looked at his watch for the fifth time in the past hour. Closing time, finally. Usually he enjoyed his busy days working at Aunt Maggie's market. The farmers were friendly, always eager to swap stories and he enjoyed the tourists too. But today, he couldn't wait to get away. Away from here and out to the peace and quiet of his boat.

Crash! Luke cursed as the top flat of strawberries he was carrying slipped from his grasp and clattered to the floor. Shiny red berries scattered freely.

"You're having a bit of an off day." Aunt Maggie grinned. "I don't remember you ever dropping anything before, even when you were really little and more in the way than not. Now in the course of one afternoon you've tried to demolish the place."

Luke knew Aunt Maggie wasn't angry. Aunt Maggie rarely got angry. Still, he knew she relied on the money the market brought her in the summer, and she couldn't very well sell squashed strawberries and broken eggs. Luke adored his eccentric great aunt. For as long as he could remember, more of his summers had been spent on his aunt's farm than with his own family in Halifax. He had never really liked the city. When Aunt Maggie's husband George had died suddenly of a heart attack two years ago, Luke knew what he wanted to do. Although he was only sixteen at the time, his parents reluctantly agreed that he could move in with Aunt Maggie and continue his schooling in the valley. They weren't keen on the idea, but Aunt Maggie had heart problems and was too stubborn to hire someone to manage the farm for her. He had been helping his great aunt with the farm and the outdoor market ever since.

Luke picked up the strawberry flats more carefully this time and put them in the cooling shed in the back of the market where they would stay fresh. "I don't know what's wrong with me today," Luke muttered somewhat sheepishly. "But don't worry. I'll cover the damages."

"Hogwash, you will!" Aunt Maggie snorted. "Anyways, you better save your money for cleaning bills. That was some fancy outfit Pete's granddaughter was wearing." Her lopsided grin teased him.

Luke groaned, wishing his aunt had not brought up the embarrassing incident. "Cleaning bills? I don't think so. I'd be surprised to see her back here any time soon."

Aunt Maggie chuckled. "You've probably got that right. From her reaction I'd say it was a new skirt. Pete has probably already dropped it off at a drycleaners. Still, it wouldn't hurt to offer to pay for the cleaning when you see her to-morrow."

"What!" Luke set down the tower of cherry boxes more suddenly than he intended.

"You drop one more flat of berries and you'll be making jam all day tomorrow, young fella."

"What do you mean, 'when I see her tomorrow'?" His dark brows squeezed into a scowl. "You're joking, right?" Luke followed his aunt as she went to get the money from the day's sales out of the till. "I'm going sailing tomorrow. It's my day off," Luke reminded Maggie, sounding more hopeful than he felt.

"Well, maybe she'd like to go with you," Maggie replied casually.

"Well, maybe she won't be invited," Luke snapped.

Aunt Maggie smiled her crooked smile, as she looked Luke straight in the eye. "She really got to you, didn't she?"

"Come on, Aunt Maggie. Give me a break. You know Miss 'High-Heels' is not my type. She'd probably hate sailing. The water would ruin her clothes and she might even break a nail!"

"Well, I don't give a horse's petutti if she's your type or not," Aunt Maggie stated flatly. "She's just arrived from Toronto and doesn't know a soul. She'd be bored silly sitting around with Reta and Pete. They're lovely people, but she's sixteen and let's face it, I'm sure she'd much rather have you for company."

"Yeah, right! Did you see the look she gave me? I'm amazed the sparks from her eyes didn't set the whole canopy on fire!"

"She'll have calmed down by tomorrow. Regardless, Reta's gonna help me do some baking for the county fair and I already told her to bring her granddaughter along."

"Who's going to run the market?"

"Mondays aren't that busy. We'll just open a bit later, that's all."

"Well, maybe she could . . ."

"No, Mr. 'I'm-Too-Embarrassed-To-Face-Her,' she's not going to help with the baking. You'll run into her sooner or later. It might as well be sooner."

Luke let out a long moan. He knew there was no changing her mind. When Aunt Maggie made a decision, nothing short of an act of God could alter it.

As they drove back to the farm, Aunt Maggie chattered on about all the latest news from the market but Luke scarcely heard a word. All he could think about was the city girl who threatened to ruin his day tomorrow. Luke had his share of attractive girls vying for his attention, so why had this one gotten to him? He still couldn't believe he'd tripped over his own feet. He had seen her from under the canopy where he was putting out some hothouse tomatoes. Dressed to kill, her honey-coloured hair gleaming in the sunlight, she seemed to float through the crowd. Man, she was hot! He lost sight of her when he got the eggs for Mrs. Brown only to find himself squeezing past her on his way to the parking lot. Their eyes met for a split second. That's when he lost it and stumbled. How could he be such a klutz? It wasn't like him at all. He could feel his cheeks getting warm just thinking about it. Her eyes. That's what did it. She had the largest, soft brown eyes. Like a fawn.

"Get a grip, buddy," Luke cautioned himself. "She's not your type."

Chapter 2

Pete White turned up the long narrow driveway. A pretty Victorian style house rose up behind the meticulously manicured lawn.

"This is it?" Sarah hadn't meant to sound so surprised, but her mother had given her the impression that the house was more like a cottage. With a name like Wolfville she hadn't dared get her hopes up.

"Home, sweet home," Pete replied. "I guess you were too little to remember it much." Her grandfather turned to face her. "We're going to have a great summer." There was a warm confidence in the old man's crinkly smile.

"I thought you were never going to get here," a tall, white-haired woman called from the doorway.

"We're comin', Reta." Sarah's grandfather winked at her as he lifted her bags out of the back of the truck. "Our stop at the market took a little longer than we expected. Had a bit of a chat with Roger and Dorothy."

"Come in, dear. Let me have a good look at you." Reta's eyes swept over the stained skirt. She may have said something about it, but Sarah was barely listening. The likeness was uncanny. The poised, confident stance, the blue-green eyes and long slender nose. Even the well-shaped lips were the same. Except for the snowy white hair and spidery lines etched into her creamy complexion, Sarah could have been looking at her mother. She had seen the occasional photograph over the years, but the marked resemblance still caught her off guard.

"You've grown into a beauty — just like your mother," her grandmother continued. "Nicole always was one to turn heads."

Sarah forced a smile. She didn't look at all like her mother.

"I'll show you to your room so you can get settled in before dinner." Sarah followed her grandmother up the narrow staircase that led to the second floor.

"It's a trifle on the small side," her grandmother said as she entered the first room at the top of the stairs. She fluffed the pillows nervously then looked around as if checking for last minute flaws.

"It's pretty," Sarah answered politely, secretly wondering how a person could even breathe in such a cramped space.

"Is there some place I could get my skirt dry cleaned?" she asked hesitantly. "I slipped on some raw eggs at the market."

"Raw eggs? Goodness. Maggie usually keeps the place pretty clean. Well, Pete can take your skirt to the dry cleaners right away. You wouldn't want to ruin it."

Her grandfather set two large suitcases beside the bed. "Your wish is my command. One more trip with the luggage and I'm off to the dry cleaners." He gave a mock salute as he went out the door.

"Just bring down your skirt when you're ready, dear," her grandmother said, closing the door behind her.

Sarah quickly changed and gave her grandfather the soiled skirt, then headed back upstairs to unpack. She flopped down on the bed. So this was it, her new summer home. It was not at all like her mother's spacious condo with its clean lines and chic furnishings. This little closet of a room was literally drenched in frills. Lace curtains hung over the windows and closet opening. The white eyelet comforter with its fussy bed-skirt was piled high with lace toss-cushions and every flat surface sported a daintily crocheted doily. Sarah had visions of being smothered by lace as she slept.

"Well, I had better get some of this unpacking done before dinner." Sarah got up from the frilly bed and pushed aside the closet curtain. How would she ever fit all of her clothes in this little cubbyhole? Then she noticed a familiar face staring down at her from the top shelf. "Raggedy Anne!"

Sarah took the doll and propped her up against the pillows on the bed. Her own Raggedy Anne doll had been given away to charity only a couple of years ago. She could still remember how furious she had been with her mother for giving it away without even asking her. She touched the stringy red strands that framed the perpetually smiling face. It was childish, but she felt oddly comforted by the floppy doll. Had her grandparents bought it for her when she was little?

After settling in, Sarah wandered downstairs. The tantalizing aroma of roast turkey reminded her that she hadn't eaten lunch. She wandered into the living room. With its ornate furniture and dark wallpaper, it reminded Sarah of pictures in history books. She checked out the tall bookcase in the corner. There were several history books including a couple of local ones. It would appear that her grandfather was a bit of a history buff. A tiny round box on the cocktail table caught her eye. Colourful strands were intricately woven in a zigzag pattern around the bottom part. The lid had a blue flower design made of diamond shapes. Something about this little trinket box seemed familiar, as if she had seen it somewhere before. She carefully opened the lid. The inside was obviously birchbark, but she couldn't figure out what the brightly coloured strands were made of.

"Pretty, isn't it?" Pete White's voice startled her.

"It's beautiful," Sarah agreed. "What is it made of?"

"Porcupine quills. The quills are dyed by hand and then

individually woven through bark to make that pattern."

"Really?" Sarah touched the delicate weaving. "The design is so intricate. How could anyone get porcupine quills to cover the whole container like that?"

Pete laughed. "With great difficulty and very sore fingers, I've heard. The Mi'kmaq people made them. In fact, there's an artist in Halifax who still makes them in the traditional way."

"Impressive." Sarah set the quill box back on the table. "It must take a long time."

"Yes, I'm sure it does. That quill box once belonged to my sister, Louise. She used to tell the queerest stories about it. When she passed away three years ago she left her special storytelling quill box to me." He turned it over and pointed to a faint signature. "That's the artist's name. It's Mi'kmaq."

"Is anybody hungry?" Reta called from the kitchen. "Dinner is ready."

"Time to carve the turkey." Pete padded off to the kitchen.

Sarah sat down at the polished mahogany table, still thinking about the quill box. Maybe her grandfather would tell her one of the strange stories sometime.

"Did you have a good year at school?" Reta asked as she settled herself at the table.

"It's summer holidays," her grandfather said. "The poor girl doesn't want to talk about school!"

"I'm sure Sarah wouldn't mind telling her own grandparents a little about herself, would you, dear?"

"I was only in school for the last month or so. Mom travelled a lot this year, so I took courses on-line and worked with Noni, my tutor."

"My word! What kind of a life is that for a young woman?"

"It works well, actually. I can work on my own schedule." For some reason Sarah felt the need to defend her mother. "I get to travel more than most kids and it gives me more time for my art."

"Hmm." Her grandmother pursed her lips together in obvious disapproval.

"What kind of art do you do?" Her grandfather's voice was kind and gentle.

"Watercolour mostly. I like to paint landscapes," Sarah answered half-heartedly.

"Well, you've come to the right place then. You can find some of the most beautiful scenery in the world in our little valley here."

"I'd love to do some painting while I'm here."

"You've got all summer." Her grandfather grinned as he stuffed a baby carrot in his mouth. "I can hardly wait to see the artist at work!"

"There are lots of interesting things to do in Nova Scotia. I'm sure you'll want to see all the sights as well," Reta suggested.

"Of course." Sarah tried to sound interested but it had been a stressful day, and she was tired. She couldn't stop replaying the scene at the market in her mind, and was grateful to her grandfather for not bringing it up.

After dinner Reta handed Sarah a tea towel. "You can dry, dear. I'll wash."

"You don't have a dishwasher?" Sarah looked around the kitchen in disbelief.

"You're the newest model." Pete White chuckled as he picked up the paper and opened to the crossword puzzle.

Sarah looked at the dishtowel in her hand as though it were a foreign object and gingerly picked up a plate. "I wanted to ask you about the Raggedy Anne doll that I found in the closet."

Reta's face softened into a smile. "Do you remember her?"

"Raggedy Anne was my favourite toy when I was little. I was surprised to find her in the closet here."

"Well, that's not much of a coincidence," her grandfather said.

"We bought her for your birthday when you were two years old." Reta looked pleased that Sarah had commented on the doll.

"I remember that day as clear as anything," Pete said. "So cute you were. You loved that doll to pieces. Never let Miss Raggedy Anne out of your sight from the moment you set eyes on her. When your mother and you left later that month, she said there was no room for the doll, that she was too big to lug around the airport, and too bulky to pack." Pete sighed. "Said she'd just buy you another one when you got to Toronto, and you'd never know the difference." His eyes moistened.

"So the doll in the closet was my very first Raggedy Anne doll." Sarah was surprised that they had kept the doll. Had they been waiting all this time for her to come back?

"Yes, dear," her grandmother answered. "I know you're a little old for dolls, but maybe you'd like to keep her for when you have a daughter some day." She let the water out of the sink and wiped off the taps. "Right now," her matter-of-fact tone signalled the end of the conversation, "I'm sure you'd like to rest. Travelling makes for a long day."

"Thank you for the wonderful dinner. It was very thoughtful of you," Sarah said, stifling a yawn. "I am a little tired. If you don't mind, I think I'll read in my room and then go to bed."

"Make yourself right at home," her grandfather said, smiling over his newspaper.

Sarah hung the damp towel on the stove handle and made her way upstairs. She was relieved to retreat to the solitude of her little room. She curled up beside her childhood friend. "I'm back, Annie. Thanks for waiting for me."

Chapter 3

The next morning Sarah woke to the aroma of sizzling bacon wafting up the stairs.

"You don't look like you're suffering from jetlag too badly," her grandfather greeted her as she walked into the kitchen. "How'd you sleep?"

"Fine, thank you."

"Don't have to be so formal, you know."

"She's just being polite, Pete. I think it's charming." Sarah's grandmother set down a plate of eggs and bacon for her.

"Well, Sunshine Sarah, it looks like our trek through time will have to wait for another day. Your grandmother already has you booked." Pete White winked mischievously.

"Our trek through time?" Sarah asked, eyebrows raised.

"To the Grand-Pré Historic Site that we talked about yesterday."

"Oh that's right. Now I remember."

"The Grand-Pré Historic Site isn't going anywhere," her grandmother commented. "And what sixteen-year-old girl would choose a bunch of historical displays over a handsome young fellow?"

Now that sounded like something her mother would say. Her grandfather leaned towards her and spoke in a loud stage whisper. "Personally, I think it's part of your grandmother's master plan to get me started on the deck she's been talkin' about for the last two years."

"What a perfect idea, Pete. I'm glad you thought of it."

Sarah's grandfather rose from the table and patted her on the shoulder. "You girls have fun today. I've got my marching orders." He grabbed his keys off the hook by the back door and headed out to the truck.

"I promised my friend Maggie that I would help her do some baking for the county fair that's coming up this weekend," Reta explained as they cleared the breakfast dishes. "We make a pretty good team. I make the crusts and she makes the filling. Maggie's great-nephew, Luke, lives with her," she continued. "I don't know how she'd ever manage without him. He's a worker, that one, and a real nice fellow, too. Maggie said he'd enjoy showing you around today while us two old ladies do our baking and catch up on the news. Do you think you could be ready in half an hour?"

"No problem," Sarah answered flatly as she made her way upstairs. So much for exploring the local history or painting in blissful solitude. Remembering the sticky heat from yesterday she chose a sundress from the closet. "Trust me, I'm not trying to impress anyone," Sarah assured Raggedy Anne, as she checked out her reflection in the full-length mirror. The floral dress moulded to her shape perfectly, flaring just above the knees. "It *is* a hot day," she said aloud as though convincing herself.

After a short drive, her grandmother pulled into a dusty lane that wound its way between waving willows to a two-storey whitewashed wooden farmhouse. The house was trimmed a bright cherry red and the barn behind was painted the same shade. Colourful wild flowers grew haphazardly in front of the verandah, which wrapped itself around most of the house. Much of the yard was left to grow wild as well.

A short, wiry woman raced out to the driveway to greet them. Her brown wrinkled face and hands betrayed her age and years in the sun, but the cornflower blue eyes peering out from under the faded ball cap sparkled with the enthusiasm of a much younger person. Sarah instantly felt drawn to this funny lady in the plaid shirt and baggy shorts that her grandmother introduced as Maggie. As the women chatted happily, Sarah wondered what this unlikely duo had in common. Her grandmother was the picture of conservative reserve in her navy slacks and matching print blouse. She carried her height regally and was well preserved for her age. She had the look of someone who lived a carefully planned, carefully executed life. It was hard to imagine her grandmother doing anything impulsive. Maggie appeared to be the complete opposite.

They entered the spacious country kitchen through the screened verandah where the aroma of freshly brewed coffee greeted them. A rugged pine table dominated the bright, sunny room, and Sarah wondered if there had once been a mob of hungry children seated on the sturdy wood chairs surrounding it. Two couches with colourful throws lined the south wall beneath large windows that overlooked the fields beyond. In the far corner of the room loomed a large stone fireplace with a couple of lumpy overstuffed chairs.

"Hope you like yer coffee strong, missy," Maggie commented to Sarah, setting a huge mug of steaming coffee on the table in front of her. "No point in drinkin' coffee if it's going to taste like day-old dishwater, I always say. And help yourself to the muffins." Maggie plunked down a basket of freshly baked banana muffins.

"Luke! Put it in high gear, our guests have arrived," Maggie yelled up the back stairs. "He's usually up with the birds. Don't know what's taking him so long today. We'll have our coffee, then you two young people can be free of us old ladies," she said to Sarah. "I'm going to put your grandma to work helpin' me bake a bunch of pies. She makes the best pie crust in the whole county." Reta smiled, pleased with the compliment.

Footsteps thumping down the stairs caught Sarah's attention. She glanced over the rim of her mug as she took another sip of the strong coffee. In the gasp that followed, Sarah inhaled the coffee, setting off an explosive coughing fit.

"Excuse me," Sarah managed to croak, setting her mug down on the table before dashing out the door to collect herself. She could feel the fire flare in her cheeks.

When her grandmother mentioned that they were going to Maggie's, Sarah should have realized that Maggie's nephew was the egg-throwing loser. Now what? How could she face this guy again? Sarah took a deep breath and tried to calm herself down. She smoothed her hair and thought about her options. There weren't any. The longer she waited, the worse it would get. She lifted her chin high and reluctantly went back in. Luke was pouring a cup of the brutal brew.

"I didn't realize you two had met," her grandmother commented.

"They had a rather unexpected meeting at the market yesterday," Maggie explained.

"*Betsy* and I are going to take a spin around Cape Split. Sarah can come if she wants," Luke offered, shrugging his shoulders. Sarah hated his glib attitude and the way he talked about her as though she weren't even there.

"*Betsy* is his boat," Maggie commented, throwing a warning glance at Luke.

"Maybe you could take Sarah on a tour of the area and

have a picnic at Cape Blomidon," Reta suggested. "She isn't really dressed for sailing today."

"I'd like sailing," Sarah replied, trying to appear composed. She didn't want her grandmother speaking for her as though she were a child. "It's a hot day. I'm sure I'll be fine."

"I don't know if sailing is a very good idea, Sarah," her grandmother clucked. "You'll be cold on the water in that skimpy sundress and you'll probably get it dirty."

"Don't worry. I'm sure we won't be gone long." Would her grandmother never stop fussing?

"The weather on the water can be chilly. I'll find you a jacket." Maggie eyed Sarah's impractical, high-heeled sandals. "And some shoes. You won't last two steps on the boat in those."

Sarah accepted a windbreaker and a rather large pair of navy canvas boat shoes from Maggie. That should make her grandmother feel better. She didn't actually have to wear them.

The drive to the marina was awkwardly silent. If her mother were here she'd have learned Luke's whole life story by now, Sarah thought. Even blaring, obnoxious music would have been preferable to this stony silence.

"You might as well change now," Luke said as they pulled into the marina parking lot.

"What?"

"The shoes." He pointed to the boat shoes Maggie had given her.

"Oh." Sarah frowned as she exchanged her elegant sandals for the scruffy overlarge blue things. She followed Luke along the boardwalk, her sundress fluttering in the breeze above the enormous blue feet, like some crazy cartoon character. If Luke was embarrassed by her odd appearance, he didn't show it. He was definitely different from other guys she had met. Perfectly in his element, he strode along the sloped boardwalk with Maggie's wicker basket swinging effortlessly by his side.

The high-pitched Scree! Scree! of the seagulls interrupted the calm as sunlight bounced off the water. Sarah breathed in deeply, tasting the salty sea air. Maybe this wasn't such a bad idea after all.

"Sarah, meet *Betsy*," Luke announced as they approached a cherry-red fibreglass boat. *Sweet Betsy* was written in large white script on her stern.

"Nice boat," Sarah commented. She had expected an older, more run-down version. This boat looked brand new.

"She's twenty-five feet of pure heaven!" Luke's dimples deepened when he smiled.

"So is *Sweet Betsy* named after someone?"

"Yes, as a matter of fact." Luke lowered himself into the cockpit. "A horse."

"You named your boat after a horse?"

"Well, *I* didn't actually name her. My great uncle George, Maggie's late husband, named her. He left me the boat when he died. Uncle George knew how much I loved sailing. Hop in and I'll tell you the story." Luke extended his hand to help Sarah climb in, but she stubbornly ignored it. She was determined to prove she was not a useless city slicker, sundress or not. Luke shook his head then disappeared into the cabin. He brought out the sail bags and carefully unfolded the mainsail. Sarah seated herself in the cockpit, happy to have stumbled on a topic of conversation.

"Uncle George was not much of a betting man," Luke began the story. "He knew too many people who had wasted all their earnings trying to get rich quick, leaving a wife and kids penniless in the process. 'Gambling is just plain stupid,' he used to say. One day some of the other farmers were badgering him to go to the horse races in Halifax. Uncle George loved horses so he finally gave in and decided to go, just to watch, of course. In the final race of the night, there was this little filly that definitely looked like she was out of her class. She was small and frail compared to the other horses, and her record wasn't too strong either. Uncle George decided then and there to put money on that little filly. 'Give her some confidence,' he said."

"Betsy?" Sarah asked, watching Luke attach the sails. Luke nodded.

"Sweet Betsy."

Sarah saw the hint of a smile around the corners of his mouth as he continued. "The other guys couldn't believe that old non-betting George was going to place money on a horse. So just for fun, they decided to add to the pot, teasing Uncle George that he could keep the money if she won. Nobody thought little Betsy stood a chance."

"Did she win?"

Luke grinned, "I guess Uncle George was right about the confidence thing because Sweet Betsy ran the race of her life, and my uncle walked away from the track $5,000 richer. So, he traded in *Strawberry*, his old sailboat, for this fancy one. Said he didn't have the energy for all the upkeep on the old one. Personally, I think the old *Strawberry* had more character, but *Sweet Betsy* is easier to steer and smoother on the water. So that's it. That's why I have a boat named after a horse."

"What a sweet story," Sarah commented.

Luke jumped onto the dock, uncleated the lines that held *Betsy* in place, and threw them inside the cabin. He pushed the boat gently backwards away from the dock and jumped aboard. Sarah was impressed with how gracefully and effortlessly he manoeuvred the boat.

The wind picked up as soon as they moved into the open water, and now they were sailing at quite a clip. For once, Sarah didn't mind the wind. She turned her face directly into it, letting her shoulder length hair blow out behind her like a golden flag. The lurching, rolling motion of the waves was exhilarating.

"We'll drop anchor on the other side of Cape Split and check out Maggie's picnic lunch," Luke suggested far sooner than Sarah would have liked. He chose a sheltered cove on the Bay of Fundy side of Cape Split and lowered the anchor. Sarah looked toward the seemingly endless ocean.

"You look like you're a hundred miles away," Luke commented.

"Just admiring the view."

Luke whistled as he spread Maggie's blue-checked tablecloth on deck and laid the food out. There were cold cuts, fresh buns, homemade muffins and strawberries. A large thermos of Maggie's super-strength coffee completed the spread.

Basking in the heat of the sun with the refreshing breeze off the water, Sarah didn't mind the long lulls in conversation. She was content to enjoy the comfortable swaying of the boat without anyone making demands of her.

"Are you ready to head back to solid ground?" Luke asked after they had eaten. "There are some strange clouds forming in the north."

"Could we just sail a little bit further into the open ocean?" Sarah asked. "Or would that be a bad idea?"

"We could sail for a few minutes further before heading back. The clouds are still a long way off."

"I'd like that."

"Let's do it!" Luke brought up the anchor and manoeuvred *Betsy* out of the sheltered cove.

Almost immediately the wind picked up. Whitecaps formed on the choppy waves. Even with the windbreaker over her lifejacket, Sarah found it chilly.

"It looks like a squall of some kind blowing in." Luke squinted toward the clouds. "We better head back." He reefed in the mainsail to make it more manageable.

"Can a squall come up that quickly? A few minutes ago there wasn't a cloud in the sky."

"Faster than you can say, 'Help I'm drowning'!"

As if proving a point, the winds suddenly grew more vicious and heavy grey clouds moved menacingly toward them. In the distance, a black veil stretched from the clouds clear down to the sea. Sarah hoped it was far away but couldn't really tell. Luke's brows furrowed as he continued to reef in the mainsail, trying not to lose control.

Before they knew it, black clouds descended, the heavens opened and torrents of rain pounded the little boat and the heaving sea.

"We'll have to motor back. This wind is too crazy," Luke yelled. "Go into the cabin." He grabbed a slicker from under the bench seat and began frantically taking the sails down, giving the wind less ammunition.

Wet and shivering, Sarah didn't need a second invitation. It was much warmer in the cabin, out of the brutal wind and relentless rain. She sat on the plush bench seat with her legs curled under her limp, soggy dress and tried to stop her teeth from chattering. She could hear Luke fighting with the sails as the boat lurched in the wind. Panic started to set in, which didn't help her already queasy stomach. What if they capsized? She certainly hoped he knew what he was doing. Finally, Luke blew in looking exhausted and nearly drowned.

"I've got us anchored in the most sheltered spot I could find." He took off the dripping slicker. "*Betsy* is pretty stable. We can hang out here until it blows over. These freak storms don't usually last very long."

"Hang out here?" Sarah asked, confused.

Luke grabbed a blanket off the double bunk at the head of the cabin and tossed it to Sarah. "Put this on. Your lips look like you've been in the blueberry patch."

Sarah gratefully wrapped herself in the blanket. "What happened to the idea of motoring back?" she asked, teeth chattering. Cold and nauseous from the constant rocking of the boat, she just wanted to get home.

"No gas," Luke answered simply.

"What!" Sarah couldn't believe it.

"We have no gas. Motors need gas to run. I don't know how to make it any clearer than that," Luke snapped.

"You brought me all the way out to the middle of the Atlantic and you have no gas? Well that's just brilliant!"

"First of all, we're not in the middle of the Atlantic, we're still in the Bay of Fundy and as I recall, you were the one who wanted to keep sailing," Luke shot back.

Despite the cold, Sarah felt heat rising to her face. How could anyone be that stupid? Nobody depends on wind. Wind is not reliable. Even she knew that.

The violent waves continued to slam *Betsy* from every

direction, convincing Sarah they would capsize any moment now. She was a strong swimmer but she was no match for the foaming ocean. Even with her life jacket on, the frigid water would swallow her whole. For the second time in as many days, Sarah found herself wishing she had never met Luke.

Luke checked the cabin to see that everything was secure, his face showing all the emotion of a stone. He grabbed a blanket and sat at the table across the cabin from Sarah. For a while neither of them spoke.

"You probably don't hear this very often, but you look terrible," Luke said, breaking the silence. "Why don't you lie down on the bunk?"

"Thanks for the compliment, but I'm fine." Sarah was determined not to be a wimp, and storm or no storm she would not cave — if she didn't throw up all over *Betsy*, that is.

"You'd be safe in the bunk if that's what you're worried about."

"What are you talking about?" Sarah asked, annoyed.

"I mean I'm not going to hit on you or anything," Luke said casually.

"What I'm worried about, is *Betsy* here capsizing and us being dumped into the freezing ocean, then sinking to a watery grave. That's what I'm worried about if you really want to know!" Sarah felt embarrassed by his comments.

"Forget it then. Sit there and be miserable," Luke muttered.

"Well, the options *are* rather limited."

Luke drummed his fingers on the table. He got up and looked out the little porthole window at the raging storm, staggered along the rocking cabin to the hatch to check once more that it was secure, then sat down and started drumming again. Sarah didn't know how long she could last in such a confined space with this caged animal.

Neither of them saw the giant wave hit. The boat lurched violently, sending Sarah flying. A sharp pain stabbed the side of her head, and then everything went black.

Through the blackness Sarah could hear frantic voices shouting but she couldn't tell what they were saying. She tried to get up but she felt dizzy and couldn't manage it. What was happening? There were people yelling and children crying. Then the voices became clearer and she realized they were speaking French. How odd. When the blackness lifted, Sarah saw a girl her age trying to get her attention. The girl was dressed in the strange clothing of an earlier time. A white apron covered her long green skirt and on her feet were wooden clogs. She clutched a grey woollen shawl around her shoulders. Her long brown hair streamed down her back beneath her white bonnet. Large, wild eyes, like those of a frightened animal, pleaded with Sarah as she stepped into a long skinny boat packed full of people. And then the scene blurred and faded away.

As the blackness enveloped her once more Sarah vaguely remembered a hand touching her cheek and a warm blanket.

Chapter 4

"Where am I?" Sarah bolted upright. Her head pounded viciously. For a moment she panicked, remembering the storm and the boat. The frilly surroundings of her room came into focus and she saw the happy face of Raggedy Anne propped up beside her.

"Welcome back. You still have eight lives left."

Sarah turned her head sharply to find Luke sitting by her bedside, his face drawn and pale. "What are you doing here?"

"Watching you sleep."

"What fun!" Sarah couldn't believe her grandparents had let him invade her privacy like that. She closed her eyes.

Maybe Luke would take the hint and leave. He was the last person she wanted to talk to right now.

"Are you okay? How do you feel?"

"Terrible, thanks," Sarah mumbled. "What happened anyway?"

"A massive wave hit *Betsy* and sent us both flying. You collided with the table and were knocked out. It was wild. Man, was I happy to see the Coast Guard." He stood up. "I'll tell your grandparents you're awake."

For the next few days Reta hovered over Sarah constantly. She wasn't even allowed to get out of bed, except to use the washroom.

"Doctor's orders," her grandmother insisted. "You have to rest as much as possible until the headaches and the nausea pass." The headaches and nausea only lasted a day, but try telling that to Sergeant Reta.

By the fourth day, Sarah thought she would go stir crazy. It was early in the morning but she was tired of sleeping. She picked up the copy of *Evangeline* from her bedside table. Her grandfather had bought the poem for her at the Grand-Pré gift shop. She hadn't realized how long it was. It was like a novel. This particular copy also included a thirty-page history of the Acadians. Sarah skimmed through the pages trying to get a sense of the situation the Acadians had been in. From the sixteen hundreds on, Acadia appeared to be at the centre of conflicts between France and England. The Acadians always remained neutral in the face of these conflicts. So why were they expelled? She read on. The beginning of the end seemed to be when the English captured the French Fort Beauséjour.

When two thousand New England troops captured Fort Beauséjour in 1755, Governor Lawrence and his Council at Halifax decided that now was the time, while these troops were in Nova Scotia and British ships were in the harbour, to settle the question of the Acadians and the oath of allegiance. Acadian deputies again refused to take the oath . . .

Sarah sighed. It was so unfair to punish people who only wanted to mind their own business and remain neutral. She turned to the beginning of the poem and began to read. As she lost herself in Longfellow's tragic tale, the plight of the Acadians pulled on her heartstrings. She couldn't help wondering if there had been a real-life Evangeline.

Sarah decided to convince her grandmother she was ready to be up and about now. She'd had enough lying around.

"Are you sure you're ready to be up?" Sarah's grandmother greeted her when she went downstairs. "Did your grandfather wake you with all his pounding out on the deck?"

"Don't worry. I've had more than enough sleep lately. I'm feeling much better today."

"Well, that's certainly good to hear." Her grandmother set down a plate full of steaming blueberry pancakes. "We've all been very worried about you. The doctor said you suffered a concussion when you fell against the table on the boat. I just knew that was a bad idea — going sailing — and you in that sundress."

Sarah wondered what the sundress had to do with the storm or the boat having no gas.

"Poor Luke feels terrible about what happened," her grandmother continued. "He's always so careful about everything. We couldn't believe he didn't check the gas before leaving. I don't think he could believe it himself. From what I hear, Maggie gave him quite the tongue-lashing about the whole thing. Well, thank goodness you're both all right. It could have been a lot worse if that Coast Guard Patrol boat had not come by when it did."

As Sarah finished eating she saw Luke come through the back gate. Here to help with the deck, no doubt. Didn't he ever have to work at the market anymore? Before she could slip up to her room her grandfather walked through the back door with Luke close on his heels.

"Look who's back to the land of the living," her grandfather teased. "You're looking much better. Got some roses back in those white cheeks of yours."

"Thanks, I am feeling better. When do you think we could visit that Historic Site that you mentioned?" Sarah asked her grandfather.

"You don't want to be too ambitious on your first day up."

"I'm very well rested, so I think I could handle it." Sarah desperately wanted to get out of the house for a bit. "If you're busy with the deck, though, we could go later in the week."

"Well, if you're sure you're up to it maybe Luke would like to take you. He's been workin' pretty steady here every day. I could do without him for the day and you two could go off to the Grand-Pré Historic Site. It'll give the guy a bit of a break from hard labour and get you out of the house. What do you think, Luke? How about bein' a tour guide today?"

"No problem." Luke grinned. "My jeep has gas and there's not a lot of water around the interpretive centre so we should be OK."

"Perfect." Sarah answered curtly, not appreciating his attempt at humour.

To Sarah's delight, in addition to the large visitor centre, there was a quaint little stone church set among swaying weeping willows and towering oaks. A bronze statue of the famous Evangeline kept watch over the lush grounds. The picturesque scene captivated Sarah so completely that she immediately forgot her resentment toward Luke.

"Is this the actual church from the deportation?"

"No. This was never a real church," Luke answered. "It was built as a memorial. The government of Canada took over the land in 1957, and in 1961 it was declared a National Historic Site. The Acadians raised money to build this church and the statue of Evangeline as a memorial to all the people who were deported. The real church would have been a simple wooden building."

Once inside the church, Sarah was amazed to see the beautiful paintings and stained glass depictions of the Acadians. The window above the door was the most interesting stained glass she had ever seen. Mostly blue to represent the ocean, it showed Acadians being shipped away from their homes. "Broken glass to symbolize broken lives," Sarah commented. "How appropriate."

"I guess so," Luke replied. "I've never really thought of it like that before."

Many of the paintings were filled with emotion as well. Sarah liked to study the faces. What were their lives really like? she wondered.

"Let's go to the main visitor centre," Luke suggested before long. "There's a lot more to see there."

"Sure." Sarah wanted to spend more time enjoying the art, but Luke was obviously ready to move on.

As they walked toward the Visitor Reception and Interpretation Centre, Sarah stopped abruptly, her eyes growing wide. There, dashing across the lawn was a girl wearing a long green skirt covered with a white apron. On her head was a white cap, and her feet were shod with wooden shoes. A shiver ran up Sarah's spine as she remembered the unusual vision she'd had on the boat that day after she had hit her head.

"What's up?" Luke asked.

"Did you see that girl in the Acadian clothes?"

Luke shrugged. "She probably works here. The guides usually wear period clothes."

That made perfect sense. Still, it was surprising that the outfit looked so similar to what the girl in her dream was wearing.

Sarah was still contemplating the unusual coincidence as they entered the Visitor Reception and Interpretation Centre.

"Bonjour," a young fellow in Acadian clothes greeted them.

"Bonjour," Sarah replied automatically.

"Hey, that reminds me," Luke said, as they entered the Exhibit Hall. "You were speaking French the other day in your sleep."

"What are you talking about?"

"When you were sleeping off the big sailing adventure. Remember? I was waiting for you to wake up, you know, in case you wanted to yell at me or something and all of a sudden you started spewing French. You were talking too fast for me to catch what you were saying, but it was definitely French. Are you bilingual?"

Sarah nodded. "Pretty much. I've had a lot of tutors and I went to a French immersion school for a while. My mother thinks a second language is critical." Sarah couldn't shake off the eerie feelings that enveloped her. First the vision on the boat and the coincidence of the Acadian girl wearing the same costume, and now some French dream that she had no memory of. Creepy.

The Exhibit Hall was larger than Sarah expected. Luke was right about there being a lot to see. There was information on the Acadian history and lifestyle, the dyke system, and of course, the *Grand Dérangement*. Sarah was reading some of the history when a guide, named Denis, announced that the movie was about to begin.

"Let's go." Luke gestured toward the theatre.

They slipped into seats near the back in time to hear Denis explain how the room was designed to resemble the hull of a ship.

"That's pretty clever," Sarah whispered.

The movie vividly portrayed the horrific events of the deportation. It was heart-wrenching to discover that, in all the confusion, families were sometimes separated. Once again, Sarah could imagine that there really had been a young woman, like Evangeline, who had been separated from the love of her life on her wedding day.

After the movie they wandered briefly through the gift shop, but Sarah wasn't in the mood for shopping. The movie had been so depressing. She didn't think she wanted additional reminders of such a horrible piece of history.

"Do you want to look around more or should we go?" Luke asked, sensing her mood.

"Let's just go. I am starting to feel a little tired."

They headed back to Luke's jeep and left for home. They were minutes away from her grandparents' place when an ambulance screamed past Luke's jeep.

"Whoa! Where did he come from?" Luke asked.

As they turned the corner, Sarah was shocked to see the ambulance parked outside her grandparents' house. Maggie's truck was out front and two paramedics were moving quickly to the door, carrying a stretcher. Sarah's heart pounded as if it would explode through her chest at any moment. She raced up the front steps, not knowing what to expect.

Paramedics tended to her grandfather in the front room. He looked weak and pale. Her grandmother and Maggie spoke in hushed tones beside him.

"What's wrong? What happened?"

"Your grandfather had a bad fall while he was working on the deck," Reta answered in a shaky voice.

"He'll be just fine," Maggie reassured her. "Pete's a tough bird."

Apparently her grandfather had tripped on a loose board on the deck. The paramedics thought he broke his left hip and possibly damaged his spine.

"I should have stayed here to help him," Luke told Maggie.

Surely he didn't think this was his fault, Sarah thought.

Her grandfather opened his eyes slightly and looked up at her, his ashen face strained. "Take care of your grandmother for me 'til I get back, won't you, kitten?" He managed a weak smile before closing his eyes again. She touched the rough, callused hand, glad that her grandfather couldn't see the tears that were about to overflow.

Chapter 5

Thunder crashed violently, rattling the windows of the old farmhouse, waking Sarah. Nautical posters and maps on the wall reminded her of her new surroundings. She had barely settled into her grandparents' house and now here she was on a lumpy sofa bed in Maggie's spare room. Her grandmother had decided to stay in Halifax so she could be close to her husband. Sarah could have stayed alone until her grandfather got out of the hospital, but no, her grandmother wouldn't hear of it.

Sarah sighed. Life on Maggie's farm had been educational, to say the least. There was no shortage of work. To her surprise, Maggie didn't hesitate to enlist her help, which included wearing rubber boots and wading through chicken poop to collect eggs, of all things. Her mother would have been absolutely mortified to see her daughter mucking through the henhouse. It was the grossest thing she'd ever had to do.

Sarah stared at the rivers of rain racing down the windows. Mother Nature was in a foul mood. Torrential rains and vicious winds pounded relentlessly against the clapboard siding. Now what? Maggie wouldn't make her go out in weather like this to collect eggs or pick berries. Maybe she would have to stand under the leaky canopy all day and sell vegetables. What a horrid thought that was. If only she had someone to make plans with or some place she could go. The pretty quill box that Sarah had brought with her from her grandparents' place caught her eye. She hoped her grandfather wouldn't mind that she had brought it with her. It made her feel closer to him, somehow. That was it! She could take the bus to Halifax and visit her grandfather in the hospital. It would be fun to go somewhere on her own and maybe she could do some shopping in Halifax while she was there.

There was a bold knock at the door, then Maggie poked her head into the room. "Good, you're awake in time for a hot breakfast. Make it snappy though, I have big plans for us today."

Make it snappy? No one had ever said that to her before. And what did Maggie mean by "big plans"? Well, she would just have to tell Maggie that she had plans of her own today.

At breakfast Maggie told Luke and Sarah that she had decided, given the weather, they would not open the market today. That's when she told them about her "clean the attic" project that she was so chipper about.

"There's stuff I haven't gone through up there since George and I bought the house some fifty years ago," Maggie had said cheerfully, as though that were something to be proud of. Although Sarah waited for the right time to tell Maggie about her idea of taking the bus into Halifax, somehow it never happened.

Reluctantly Sarah followed Luke up the steep, narrow steps that led to the attic of Maggie's rambling farmhouse. His songbird whistling grated on her nerves. Apparently the weather hadn't dampened his spirits.

"Unbelievable!" Sarah wrinkled her nose at the endless sea of clutter in the musty attic. Piles of junk stretched from one end to the other, covered with cobwebs and dust. For the briefest second she considered telling Maggie to forget it. But as soon as the thought flitted through her mind, Sarah knew that she wouldn't do it. Maggie was unlike anyone she had ever met.

"What are you smiling about?" Luke flashed her a strange look.

"I was just thinking about when Maggie sat in the bucket of berries yesterday."

"Yeah, that must have been a sight."

Sarah had gone with Maggie to pick raspberries from the bushes at the back of the house. Maggie slipped on a patch of wet grass and fell smack into her bucket of berries, squashing them into juice and staining her already colourful shorts. They both laughed until tears rolled down their cheeks. Sarah was so doubled over with laughter that she could hardly help Maggie out of the bucket. The memory of the ridiculous incident warmed Sarah. She couldn't picture her glamorous mother or prim grandmother sitting in a bucket of raspberries. And if they were, she was quite sure they wouldn't be laughing. Sarah sighed. She couldn't disappoint the warm, if demanding, Maggie.

"What is it Maggie wants us to do up here?" she asked weakly.

"Organize, toss, clean-up. You know."

But she didn't know. She didn't have a clue. She had never even cleaned her own bedroom. Luke was already poking around some of the boxes, stirring up dust. "By the looks of things we should be finished some time next year," Sarah groaned.

"Aunt Maggie's spring cleaning *is* a little overdue," Luke agreed.

"Just a tad." She pulled her silky hair into a ponytail and put on the rubber gloves Maggie had given her. Even so, she didn't intend to touch anything up here.

Once they got started it wasn't as bad as Sarah had feared. The steady rhythm of the rain beating on the roof was oddly comforting. After a while she didn't even notice the musty smell, and the "junk" proved to be interesting. She found an ornate pair of badly oxidized candlestick holders that she put aside for polishing later. She was sure they were real silver or at least silver plate. She dusted off an old photograph of Maggie and her late husband. Sarah was surprised that Maggie, while not what you would call pretty, was fashionable and sophisticated-looking in her youth.

Luke wandered over from his corner of the attic dragging two bulging garbage bags.

"So where's the stuff you're throwing out?" he asked, eyeing the neat little pile of odds and ends that Sarah had meticulously dusted.

"This stuff is fascinating, Luke. Besides," Sarah fingered her treasures defensively, "it's not up to me to decide what to pitch. It's not my stuff."

"Oh brother," Luke groaned, "we'll never get anywhere at this rate."

They decided to organize everything into labelled boxes for Maggie to deal with later. It was all junk, according to Luke, except for the picture of Maggie and George.

Other than Luke's incessant whistling, and the occasional comment, they worked in silence. Sarah appreciated Luke's undemanding presence. It was better than being asked a million questions about a nonexistent father or her glamorous television mother. A twinge of self-pity niggled at the back of Sarah's mind as she wondered what it would be like to have a regular family with a father and a mother who had normal jobs. Her thoughts drifted back to her grandfather. Maybe she would take the bus to Halifax tomorrow.

Sarah spied a large black steamer trunk half hidden under old blankets and quilts. She dumped the blankets to the floor. The trunk looked intriguing with its tarnished brass trim and rusted old padlock. Sarah had never seen such a strange lock. It was large with a keyhole for an old fashioned skeleton key. She pulled at the lock in hopes that it would open, but without luck.

"Luke, what do you think is in here?" Sarah hoped Luke would take the hint and help her open it.

"More junk." Luke continued to load some old dishes into a box.

"Maybe not. I think we should open it and find out. It looks mysterious."

Luke rolled his eyes. "It looks like the trunk I have in my room that I used to move all my stuff from Halifax. And I keep junk in it." Luke picked up a board that was lying beside the window and tried to pound the lock free. It didn't budge.

"We'll ask Maggie about it later." Luke set down the piece of wood. "She must know what's in there."

"I guess we don't have much choice." Still, Sarah hated to give up so easily. "Be right back." She raced downstairs to her room and grabbed a wire hanger from the closet. Maybe she could pick the lock.

After several clumsy attempts Sarah tossed the hanger

aside. "Do you think the key is up here somewhere?" she called to Luke who was stuffing a broken lamp into the trash bag.

"Could be." Luke straightened up and looked vaguely around the attic. "But finding it in here would be like the old 'needle in the haystack' scenario."

Sarah surveyed the piles and boxes they hadn't even touched yet. Luke was right. It would take forever to go through all this stuff, and they didn't even know if the key were here. It had probably been lost years ago. Disappointed, Sarah wandered over to the tiny window. The dreary grey sky offered little hope that the pouring rain would quit any time soon, although it was not coming down as hard as before.

The small casement window looked out over the dyke and reclaimed marshland that Sarah's grandfather had pointed out on her first day in Nova Scotia. It was amazing to think that hundreds of years earlier an Acadian woman may have looked out her window as her husband and neighbours piled up logs and sod to build the dyke. Sarah squinted through the mist that hung over the valley. A figure, barely visible through the greyness, walked along the top of the dyke. Who would be out in this weather? Green fabric twisted in the wind and the girl — Sarah could tell now that it was a girl — held a shawl tightly around her for protection. What would the young woman from the historic site be doing walking along the dyke in this downpour?

At that moment, the girl looked up and waved as though

she had just caught sight of someone she knew. Maybe she was meeting someone. But no one else was anywhere in sight. And then she was gone — faded into the mist. Sarah rubbed her eyes and looked more closely. There was no sign of the girl anywhere. She must be losing her mind.

"Waiting for the rain to stop?"

Sarah jumped at the sound of Luke's voice. She had been so focused on the young woman on the dyke that she hadn't noticed him standing beside her at the window.

"Whoa! Somebody's a little jittery. What's up?"

"How long have you been standing there?"

"Sorry, I didn't know I needed permission to look out the window."

Sarah ignored the remark. "Did you see anyone walking on the dyke? I thought I could see someone."

"Are you crazy? Who would be out in this?"

Sarah wished she hadn't said anything to Luke. "I think I need some fresh air." She tugged as hard as she could on the window but it refused to budge. Finally, with Luke's help, she managed to pry the window open enough to let some air in. She pulled back the thick brown curtains and something clattered to the floor. There at her feet was a large, iron skeleton key.

Luke picked the key up off the floor and inspected it more closely. "It looks like a needle to me. What do you think?"

"Do you think it's the key to the trunk?" Sarah felt a tingle of excitement.

"There's only one way to find out." Luke handed Sarah the key.

She held her breath as she slid the key into the lock and turned it. A perfect fit!

"Looks like this is your lucky day!" Luke grinned. "Maybe you should go out and buy a lottery ticket."

She lifted the lid slowly as though expecting something to jump out at her. The trunk was full of old books.

"Hmm, maybe this is interesting junk after all," Luke commented. Sarah had already started wading through the books. Most of them were old history books. A dull red hard cover book caught her attention. The title *The Acadian Exiles* was barely visible in faded gold letters. "Do you think Maggie would mind if I borrowed this?" Sarah asked. "My grandfather talks about the Acadians all the time."

"I don't see why not."

Sarah put the book aside and continued to dig through the trunk. Luke, meanwhile, was already sorting through another box. Sarah dutifully closed the trunk. Looking through the old books was much more appealing, but she couldn't very well leave all the work to Luke.

By the end of the afternoon, "spiders' paradise" had been transformed into a semi-neat, organized storage room with not a dust ball in sight, thanks to Luke. Sarah found herself pushing things from spot to spot, not accomplishing much of anything. She couldn't get the lone figure on the dyke out of her mind.

After the final sweep of the afternoon, Sarah took *The Acadian Exiles* to her room to read. She curled up on her bed and flipped through the chapters, stopping at the chapter titled "The Expulsion of the Acadians." After the movie at the Interpretation Centre, Sarah had thought a lot about the Acadians. She discovered that the naïve Acadians were totally oblivious to their imminent expulsion.

Sarah skimmed through the chapter, reading about Lawrence, the newly appointed governor, and how he was determined to get rid of the Acadians. She then came across a shocking piece of information. Lawrence and the Halifax council proceeded with plans for the expulsion without the authority or the knowledge of the home government. England had known nothing about Lawrence's plans. Sarah closed the book. This was too distressing for an already dismal day. She took the little quill box from the dresser beside the bed and ran her fingers over the delicate pattern as she wandered over to the window. It wasn't raining now and she had been cooped up in the house all day. Maybe a walk would do her good.

Sarah slipped out the door still clutching the tiny quill box in her hand. The ground was wet and mucky as she crossed through the fields and she was glad that she had decided to pull on the hideous rubber boots Maggie had bought her. Before she knew it she had reached the dyke. She walked along the top feeling the chill of the humid air. A shiny round stone wedged in the mud caught her eye. She bent over and picked it up. It was smooth with a glassy, reddish colour. Sarah decided to keep the shiny stone as a souvenir. She pulled the lid off the quill box and was about to put the stone inside when a strong wind came out of nowhere. The icy cold fingers of the wind gripped her and sliced through her flesh like needles. It whipped wildly at her hair and clothes, and Sarah felt herself becoming dizzy. Frantically she reached out to grab onto something but there was nothing to grab. Finally the roar of the wind trailed off in the distance, and Sarah felt herself falling slowly as though the wind had spent its anger and was trying to set her down gently, like a leaf fluttering to the ground.

She opened her eyes. Where was the special trinket box? She must have dropped it when the crazy wind caught her by surprise. Her grandfather would never forgive her if she lost it. She looked along the dyke trying to find it. That's when she noticed she wasn't alone. Standing beside her was the Acadian girl wearing the green skirt and white cap.

Chapter 6

Was she dreaming? She had never seen the girl up close, yet Sarah recognized the face from her dream immediately. The owl-like brown eyes fringed in long black lashes dominated the delicate pixie face. Now they scrunched together as the petite girl squinted suspiciously at Sarah.

"Who are you? Are you a ghost?"

Sarah understood the lilting words to be French although the dialect was strange. The girl chattered on, not waiting for an answer. It was difficult to catch all the words, which fell in a steady torrent like water over a waterfall. She was saying something about Sarah sneaking up on her. By the time she finally stopped to take a breath, Sarah's head was spinning.

"I'm Sarah," she said tentatively in French. "Who are you?"

"My name is Anne LeBlanc. I live in the farm over there." Sarah's eyes followed where the girl was pointing. It was precisely where Maggie's farm should have been. The sun peeked over the horizon, streaking the morning sky with pink and orange hues in a beautiful sunrise — one worth painting. But Sarah couldn't think about watercolours right now. Her legs wobbled and a shiver fluttered along her spine. She drank in the salty sea breeze that blew in from the basin. Never before had a dream been so vivid or so real.

"So, Sarah," Anne said, staring at her, "if you're not a ghost, who are you? Where do you live and how did you get here? I've never seen anyone dressed in such a way."

Sarah found the rapid-fire speech exhausting to listen to, but at least the French girl named Anne didn't expect many answers to her endless questions and ramblings.

"Ow!" Sarah cried, touching her hand to her face where Anne had unexpectedly reached over and pinched her cheek.

"You are not a ghost then, or I wouldn't be able to pinch you like that."

"Of course I'm not a ghost and that wasn't a nice thing to do," Sarah answered angrily. Anne laughed, which made her even angrier. "What's so funny?"

"You!" Anne continued giggling. "You're dressed in those silly clothes and when you talk — it's so funny! I'm sorry but I couldn't help it. Maman says I must learn to show more self-control if I expect François to marry me."

"You're getting married? How old are you?"

"Almost eighteen," Anne said proudly. "On my eighteenth birthday François and I will get married — if he remembers to ask Papa, that is."

Sarah didn't hear what else Anne said about François. She was still thinking about the marriage thing. The petite Acadian girl looked much younger than eighteen but still, who would want to get married at eighteen?

"Would you like to come with me? I can't talk all day. Maman won't be happy to find out the goats aren't milked or the eggs gathered and Papa will be looking for breakfast soon."

Anne skipped across the top of the dyke, leaving Sarah little choice but to follow. She clomped along behind in the clumsy rubber boots, feeling ridiculous. The boots were definitely not needed this morning. "This *morning*," Sarah whispered the words to the golden sun that was now fully visible on the horizon and shook her head in disbelief. The dry ground held no signs of the incredible rainstorm. Too weird!

Anne turned suddenly, a frown creasing her brows as though she were thinking hard about something. "You didn't tell me where you live."

"I'm a guest at Maggie Hébert's house."

"The Héberts are my neighbours, but there's no *Magee* around here," Anne stated emphatically. "I should know. I've lived here all my life."

Confused, Sarah followed Anne along the edge of an empty field and through a stand of trees. Anne chirped away, like a wind-up toy that never wound down, so Sarah gave up trying to follow what she was saying.

As they came into the clearing, Sarah stopped and stared. "Oh my gosh!" she remarked out loud. There in front of her, where Maggie's house should have been, was a cottage that looked very similar to the ones in the displays at the Grand-Pré National Historic Site.

At the sound of the English words, Anne's cheerfulness quickly evaporated. "You're English!" she accused. "That's why you sound so funny." The bubbly banter had turned to a sneer.

"What year is it?" Sarah asked ignoring the questions and accusations. She had to find out what was going on.

"*Beh!* 1755, of course. You must be sick in the head or something. You don't know where you live and you don't know what year it is!" Anne clicked her tongue and shook her head as if she felt sorry for Sarah.

Sarah hardly noticed. Had she somehow gone back in time? That was impossible, wasn't it? Then it hit her like a tidal wave. The deportation of the Acadians was in 1755. If she had somehow gone back in time she was in a lot of trouble.

Anne motioned for Sarah to follow her as she rushed past the cottage and headed toward the thatched-roof barn. Sarah wrinkled her nose at the smell and gingerly stepped around the generous evidence that horses had recently passed this way. Young willows waved their branches in greeting from either side of the trail.

It was amazing how quickly Anne could move in her wooden clogs. Sarah found it hard to keep up in her clumsy boots. Goats bleated in the rough enclosure beside the barn and she sincerely hoped that Anne was not expecting her to milk any goats.

The stench of manure and sweaty animals seemed over-powering to Sarah as they entered the barn. This was not at all like Maggie's place. With the exception of the chicken coop, Maggie's farm smelled of sweet berries and wild-flowers. A lump formed in Sarah's throat and her eyes began to fill. What would she do now? And what would Anne's family do if they found out she was English? This was such a mess. Sarah had never felt more alone in her life. Somehow she had to get back to Maggie's farm.

"What's wrong? Are you sick? Maybe I should call Maman. She would know what to do. She can work won-ders with herbs." Anne's large brown eyes were warm and friendly once more.

"No, don't call your mother. I have to tell you something important. Can you keep a secret?"

"Of course!" Anne's eyes brightened at the mention of a secret.

"You keep asking me where I'm from," Sarah started slow-ly. "Somehow I came here from the future — many, many years from now. It's hard to believe. I don't quite believe it myself. But if it is 1755 as you say, then it must be true. I live, or at least I did live, in the year 2007."

Anne gasped. "*Non! Pas possible!*"

Sarah took a deep breath and continued, "I was standing on the dyke, holding a little trinket box. Suddenly, everything went black. There was a vicious wind so strong I thought I was being thrown into the air. Next thing I knew you were standing beside me on the dyke and Maggie's farm had vanished. Look at these stupid things." Sarah pointed to her sloppy rubber boots. "Where could you get these in 1755? And these clothes are all stitched by fancy machines," she continued. "People don't sew clothes by hand anymore."

Anne's mouth fell open, but for once the petite French girl was speechless.

Sarah continued, "I do speak English, but I'm not from England. I came from Nova Scotia, at a different time."

"Nova Scotia!" Anne spat the words out. "Yes, that's what the English call it now, but we still call it L'Acadie."

"I'm not a spy or anything. I would never hurt you or your family." Sarah hoped Anne believed her.

"We'll be friends, then," Anne said slowly. "Your story is *très bizarre*. I don't know if it can be true, but I have a good feeling about you. I think you mean no harm. Don't tell Maman your strange story. She gets very upset with things she doesn't understand. It'll be our secret, *oui*?"

Sarah nodded in agreement, relieved that Anne was smiling once more.

"Now I'll need to get you some clothes. That won't be easy." Anne clicked her tongue again. "You're so much taller than I am. I know! I'll bring you the special skirt I wore at my brother Philippe's wedding. It's longer than this one. It'll have to do. You can't wear what you have on." Anne threw her hands up in the air as she rushed out the barn door.

Sarah nervously wrung her hands as she waited for Anne. *Bizarre*, Anne had called her story. *Bizarre* didn't begin to describe how Sarah felt.

A few moments later, Anne blew through the door clutching an armful of clothes. She handed Sarah an indigo blue skirt with a matching lace-up top that was like a jacket. There was also a white blouse with long frilly cuffs. "Tonight I'll try to find some old cloth to make into a skirt for you. *Vite!* Get dressed! We have much work to do. Here are Papa's moccasins. They're the only ones that will fit you. I'll start milking the goats." She tossed the moccasins on the dirt floor and skittered out the door.

Sarah barely squeezed into the pretty flounced skirt and frilly blouse. The outfit didn't look like what you would wear traipsing around the fields, but all things considered it was a whole lot better than blue jeans. She hid her own clothes under the hay then combed her hair with her fingers. "Ready or not," Sarah whispered under her breath as she left the safety of the barn.

The yellow warmth of the sun helped raise Sarah's spirits. She wondered if Luke or Maggie had missed her yet. A piercing scream interrupted her thoughts.

"Maman! Maman!" A little girl appeared over the grassy slope running toward the house.

"Something's wrong!" Anne yelled as she raced toward the child. At the same time a woman dashed out of the house, wiping her hands on her apron.

"*Le Bon Dieu!* What is it, *ma petite*? What has happened? Where is Jean-Paul?"

Sarah followed them down a grassy slope and into the woods. There must have been an accident. Sunlight filtered through the trees painting criss-cross patterns on the path as she ran toward the voices. It didn't take her long to reach them. The woman sat by the water, her dress wet and muddy. From the look of the limp child in her arms, Sarah guessed that she had just pulled the little boy out of the river. She quietly approached them. The woman rocked back and forth, tears streaming down her face.

"He's dead. My poor little boy is dead. God, why did you need to take another son from me? Was one not enough?" Anne and her little sister huddled together beside them. Anne stroked the long dark hair of the little girl, trying to calm her gasping sobs.

Sarah knelt down beside them, looking closely at the young boy, searching for signs of life. Then she took courage and said, "I may be able to help your son."

"Yes, please help him," the woman pleaded. "Anne, take Jeanne to the house. She should not be here to see her little brother like this."

Sarah had never used her CPR training in a real-life crisis. She hoped with all her heart that her lifeguard training would not fail her now. Sarah took the limp body from the sobbing mother and laid him on the ground. She wished she had a blanket or something to put under him but at least the ground was dry. She tilted the little head back and breathed short warm breaths into the lifeless form. The woman knelt next to her son clutching her rosary beads. Sarah continued the rhythmic puffs, watching closely for any signs of life. If only she could dial 9-1-1. But it was useless to think about that. It was all up to her. Sarah was beginning to wonder how much longer she could keep it up when the delicate black-fringed eyelids fluttered slightly. *God, please let him live.* She kept up the steady rhythm of warm breaths into the small body. She felt the little body jerk and then Jean-Paul hiccuped, spewing what seemed to Sarah like half the river. His mother shrieked and cried and laughed all at the same time. Sarah held the boy for a moment then stepped back to allow his mother to clasp her little son closely.

Feeling exhausted, she sat down on a rock and held her head in her hands. She had done it. It was an unbelievable, overwhelming feeling. She had never felt better in her whole life.

"What can I ever do to thank you?" The tear-stained face was smiling now. She held her small son close to her chest. "I'm Madame LeBlanc. And you? Does Jean-Paul's guardian angel have a name?"

Sarah smiled. "*Je m'appelle Sarah*. I'm glad I was able to help."

Madame LeBlanc gently touched her shiny hair. "You are not from around here, and you arrive just when Jean-Paul is drowning." She smiled and winked at Sarah, then leaned over close. "But we won't tell anyone, except my husband, of course. He would want to know that our houseguest is one of God's divine helpers. Come! Tonight there will be a great celebration." She scooped Jean-Paul into her arms and led the way back to the cottage.

Chapter 7

The pungent smell of stew from the heavy black pot hanging over the fireplace awakened Sarah's hunger. How long had it been since she had last eaten? Anne ladled out generous servings to Sarah and her younger sister, Jeanne. Sarah helped herself to a bun from the basket in the centre of the table.

"Ow!" Sarah held the side of her face where her teeth jarred against the surprisingly hard bun.

Anne burst out laughing. "It's a good thing something woke you up. I've been asking you questions about how you rescued Jean-Paul and you haven't even heard a word I've said."

"Anne, do not speak like that." Maman's voice was firm as she bustled around the large room, which appeared to be kitchen, living room and bedroom rolled into one. "It's bad luck. The angels don't owe us an explanation."

"Angels? What angels?" Anne asked, her eyebrows arching sharply. Sarah shrugged her shoulders. She didn't know how to explain what Madame LeBlanc thought.

Maman went on to tell how nothing short of a miracle could have brought back her son. How God sent Jean-Paul's very own *ange gardienne* to answer her prayers. "*Le Bon Dieu!* I will never forget this day." Maman looked heavenward as she made the sign of the cross. Sarah knew that she too would never forget this day. She watched Jean-Paul for a moment as he slept, nestled safely in the middle of the bed, and felt her heart swell. It was all surreal.

"Maman, when will Mathieu be home?" Jeanne asked as she finished her bowl of stew. "He promised to help me and Jean-Paul build a fort, but he's never around."

"He's gone with Papa to help your brother Philippe build his new barn," Maman answered, as she kneaded dough. "Mathieu is almost a man now, *ma petite*. He has to learn to do a man's work." Maman smiled at her young daughter. "Jean-Paul must rest this afternoon. No fort building today. There's much to prepare for our celebration tonight," Maman continued. "Jeanne, you go with Anne to find some fat blueberries. You know how much Papa likes blueberries. That'll be the best part of the meal." Maman's round face smiled warmly at her youngest daughter.

Jeanne's face brightened at this suggestion. "Can Sarah come too?"

"If she would like to."

Jeanne jumped off the wooden bench, her chubby braids bouncing behind her. "Papa loves a feast." Jeanne took a birchbark basket down from a shelf on the wall.

"Of course," Maman responded. "What man doesn't love a feast?" Maman's whole body chuckled at this comment. "And won't they be surprised to meet Jean-Paul's pretty *ange gardienne!*" Maman made the sign of the cross again.

"This has been quite a day for you so far," Anne said, after they left the cottage. "First I think you're a ghost, and then Maman thinks you're an angel!" Anne paused for a moment and then gave Sarah a strange look. "Maybe you *were* sent here to rescue Jean-Paul."

"That's crazy!" Sarah wrinkled her forehead. "You sound like your mother now. You know I'm not an angel. Don't you?"

Anne shrugged. "I think so. But I don't know how you got here and you *did* bring Jean-Paul back to life. How do you explain that?"

Jeanne grabbed Sarah's hand and pulled her towards the woods. "Let's run, Sarah. We'll race Anne to the blueberry bushes."

"Leave her alone," Anne admonished her little sister. "You're like a pesky black fly. I want to show Sarah where Ti-Pierre is buried."

Jeanne kept her grip on Sarah's hand but stopped running. Anne paused beside the large willow and pointed to a small white cross that was placed beneath it.

"He should have been buried behind the church, but Maman said he was too young to be so far away from his mother, so Papa buried him here."

"What happened?" Sarah asked quietly, recalling Madame LeBlanc's words about another son that God had taken from her.

"No one knows." Anne hung her head sadly. "He died when he was only a few weeks old. He fell asleep and never woke up. Poor Maman. She has never been the same since."

"That's sad about your baby brother, Anne," Sarah sympathized.

"Hurry up you two." Jeanne tugged on Sarah's hand. "We'll never have enough blueberries for Papa if we stand here all day."

"She's right. And Maman will need our help when we get back." Anne's face lit up. "I think she is going to invite the Héberts over tonight."

"Anne's going to marry François. I even saw them kissing behind the barn once." Jeanne puckered her lips and made smacking sounds.

"Jeanne! How could you say such a thing? We were not kissing. He was telling me about his new horse." Anne glared at her little sister.

"You were kissing! You were kissing!" Jeanne skipped in circles around her sister still making faces.

"See — what a pest!" Anne gestured toward her sister.

After that, Anne ignored her little sister and Jeanne finally got bored with the teasing. Anne never ran out of topics of conversation, and even while they were busy picking berries she hardly stopped for a breath. It was so much fun that Sarah almost forgot about everything else. Almost. The sweet song of the birds as they flitted from tree to tree reminded her of Luke's whistling. By now someone would have noticed she was missing. Her poor grandfather. As if he didn't have enough problems.

Sarah wanted to run to the dyke right then. She didn't know how to get back home but the dyke was her only connection. There had to be a way back to her own century. Sarah sighed. It would be impossible to sneak away right now. And when she thought about it, she didn't want to miss the Acadian celebration. She'd slip away after they ate, before it got dark.

As they came in view of the cottage after picking berries, Anne's father and her brother were just returning from the barn raising.

"Papa! Papa!" Jeanne greeted her father as though he had been away for days, rather than a few hours. Berries flew out of her basket, which swung wildly by her side.

Sarah watched as Monsieur LeBlanc scooped up the excited Jeanne. One of her tiny wooden clogs flew off as he danced around with her in his arms. He was not a tall man. His thin, rugged face was tanned and etched with deep lines, smile lines, Sarah decided, as she watched him play with Jeanne.

Anne linked her arm in Sarah's. "You may be Jean-Paul's angel but Jeanne is Papa's angel. Papa, come and meet my friend," she called to her father.

"Sarah brought Jean-Paul back from the dead," Jeanne added.

"What's this about Jean-Paul?" Monsieur LeBlanc extended his hand toward Sarah.

"It was a miracle, Papa." Anne's voice was full of admiration. "He fell into the river and by the time we got to him he wasn't breathing, but Sarah breathed into his mouth and saved him."

Monsieur LeBlanc suddenly looked very serious. "Is this true? You saved my son from the river?"

Sarah nodded. Soon Madame LeBlanc was out on the front step telling her version of the story. Everyone seemed to be talking at once.

"Mathieu!" Papa called. "Come here. Meet our special guest." He turned and faced Sarah once more. "Words are not enough at a time like this."

Sarah smiled shyly. She understood exactly what he meant.

Madame LeBlanc excitedly repeated the story for Mathieu, who appeared less than impressed.

"If she is Jean-Paul's guardian angel, why is she wearing Anne's clothes?" he sneered. "Isn't that the dress Anne wore to Philippe and Monique's wedding?"

Everyone fell silent. All eyes turned toward the sullen boy who leaned against the cottage chewing on a piece of grass, then Madame LeBlanc looked at Sarah as though she hadn't noticed the clothes before now.

"Sarah never said she was an angel," Anne said. "I found her wandering around the dyke by herself. She was confused and all alone. I think her family may have been killed in the raid at Port Royal. Her clothes were terrible," Anne continued dramatically. "Of course I gave her what I could."

Sarah noticed that Anne told this clever story without so much as the blink of an eye, and while she appreciated Anne's helping her out of the awkward moment, she realized she knew nothing about Port Royal. She didn't even know where it was. What if they asked her something about it, or about her family? Her lips started to quiver.

"She saved my son from the river," Monsieur LeBlanc stated. "That's good enough for me." He turned to Sarah. "We'll never forget this day. You're an honoured guest in our home for as long as you wish to stay. And tonight we celebrate! Now, I'll go see my little man who almost left us today."

Chapter 8

Sarah helped Jeanne lay out the heavy pewter plates, as Anne and her mother loaded food onto the large pine table. There were meat pies, roasted vegetables and nuts, fresh bread and molasses, and jugs of spruce beer. Sarah was impressed, especially considering the rustic surroundings. Was all the food prepared over an open fire? Her mother found frying eggs and bacon a challenge, even with all her modern appliances.

Soon the entire LeBlanc family gathered around the table with the parents like bookends at either end. As Monsieur LeBlanc said a special blessing to honour her, Sarah felt the love and warmth that permeated this home. She had known them for such a short time and yet they had welcomed her as though she were part of the family.

The meat pies called *pâtés* tasted delicious. They reminded Sarah of a dish she loved to order in her mother's favourite restaurant in Paris. "Did you bake the *pâtés* over the fire?"

Everyone burst into laughter and Madame LeBlanc repeated the question over and over as though she thought it was the funniest thing she had ever heard. Sarah's cheeks burned with embarrassment. Finally Anne stopped laughing long enough to tell her that they were baked in the outdoor oven.

"Just ignore them," said Monsieur LeBlanc coming to her rescue. "I could tell you stories of their foolishness that would take until next year!" He spread his arms wide in a dramatic gesture. "Do you remember the time I asked you if you wanted to go ice fishing with me?" he asked Mathieu. "You thought we were going to catch ice." Monsieur LeBlanc's deep voice rumbled in laughter and Jeanne giggled until she almost fell off her chair. "You were so proud of yourself when you brought in some chunks of ice from the edge of the river!"

"I was only four years old, Papa!" Mathieu protested.

Madame LeBlanc served a thick milk-custard dish topped with the wild blueberries for dessert. As they finished the meal, sounds of laughter and children's voices descended on the cottage.

"It's François' family," Anne whispered to Sarah, beaming happily. "They've come to celebrate with us. I knew Maman would invite them."

Noise filled the tiny cottage as a steady stream of kids poured in and friends greeted each other. Monsieur Le-Blanc waved to Sarah. "Come, *ma belle ange*. Meet our good friends."

Monsieur Hébert was stockier than Anne's father and a little taller. His rosy face glowed with joie de vivre as he took Sarah's hand. The mother of the noisy tribe was a short, round woman with a wide, friendly smile. She smothered Sarah in a warm hug before bustling over to help clear the table.

Sarah spotted François immediately. He swung through the door with an air of confidence, smiling brightly at the sight of Anne who was positively glowing.

"Isn't he good-looking?" Anne whispered to Sarah, nodding in François' direction. "I hope he talks to Papa tonight. He said he would the next chance he got."

"Stop your mindless chatter, Anne," her mother chided. "No one wants a lazy wife. Get the water for these dishes or François will be back home sound asleep before you are ready to visit."

"*Oui, Maman*." Anne grinned as she fastened the empty buckets to the wooden yoke and hoisted the contraption onto her slim shoulders.

The Hébert children had already made themselves at

home and seemed to be everywhere. The youngest, Gabriel, was a four-year-old ball of energy who raced circles around his tired-looking maman. Marie-Claire appeared to be close in age to Jean-Paul. The eight-year-old twins, Joseph and Martin, took great enjoyment in teasing Jeanne and pulling her braids, which she certainly didn't discourage.

Sarah stepped outside to escape the crowd for a moment. The light of the full moon filtered through a veil of wispy cloud. The moon always filled Sarah with a sense of awe, and tonight was no different. "Where are you, Luke and Maggie?" she whispered to the stars. "Are you out there somewhere? Are you worried about me?"

As she wandered toward the back of the house she pondered the interesting coincidence of the name Hébert, but Mathieu's angry voice interrupted her thoughts.

"You aren't telling the truth, Anne. You think you have everyone fooled but I know better. I can see it in your face. Who is this strange girl?" He wagged his finger in her face. "An angel? Ha! You don't have me fooled for a moment."

Sarah held her breath as she ducked behind the large willow before they noticed her.

"I told you, *imbécile*! She's not an angel. You know what Maman is like."

"Well your friend isn't from Port Royal either, or if she is, she's the daughter of an English soldier. She doesn't talk the way we do, and I've watched her. Half the time she doesn't even know what's going on. I tell you, sister, she's not to be trusted. She may have all of you under her spell, but she's not fooling me." With a toss of his head he went back to the house.

Sarah came out from behind the tree, her knees shaking. "I heard what Mathieu said."

"Whew! You scared me!" Anne set the buckets down. "Don't mind Mathieu. He was born on a stormy day in January, and Maman says he's had a storm cloud following him ever since. He's harmless. He sounds like a wolf, but he's really a mouse — a very lazy mouse." Anne groaned as she picked up the yoke attached to the heavy water buckets once more.

Fiddle music flowed through the open door. "Papa is the best fiddler in all of Grand-Pré," Anne said proudly. "I love to dance. Don't you?"

The table and benches had been pushed against the wall and several of the little ones were twirling to the lively music. François held wooden spoons back-to-back and clapped out the rhythm on his knees.

"You are as slow as molasses in January!" Maman clucked, taking the buckets of water from Anne. "Such a dawdler!"

But tonight nothing could upset the good-natured Anne. She grinned at Sarah as she helped her mother dump the water into the large pot hanging over the fire.

"Where have you been?" Jeanne grabbed Sarah's hand pulling her to the centre of the floor where several of the children were dancing. "I've been looking for you."

Sarah felt self-conscious dancing to the strange music. Everyone's feet moved so quickly. But the rhythm of the music proved irresistible and soon she was twirling and tapping her toes to the music along with the others. Even the snarly Mathieu appeared to be having fun. Exhausted, Sarah finally sat down, happy to watch for a while.

"This is for you." Jean-Paul was at her elbow with a cup of spicy cider.

Sarah smiled as she took the cup from him. "What a thoughtful boy you are."

He crawled up on the bench beside her, adoration shining in his saucer-like chocolate eyes. Warmth washed over Sarah as she wrapped her arm around the little boy. He was here right now because of her. If she lived to be a hundred, she'd never forget that feeling.

The fiddle music slowed to a haunting melody and everyone stopped their frenzied dancing to listen to the sad story the fiddle was telling. Sarah's joy over rescuing Jean-Paul dissolved into sadness as she thought of the bitter deportation that was in store for these loving, gentle people. When the last note sounded, Monsieur Hébert stood and moved toward the large stone fireplace.

"Time for a story, *mes petites*," he announced.

"Tell us about the *Chasse-galerie*, Papa," his daughter Marie-Claire pleaded, her cherub face aglow from the fire.

"*Oui! Oui! La Chasse-galerie!*" the others chanted.

Everyone gathered around for the story. Marie-Claire

and Jeanne curled up together on the braided rug with Jean-Paul snuggled in front of them, his head on Jeanne's lap. Anne motioned for Sarah to join her on a large chest. "Look. François and Papa are going for a walk," she whispered, barely able to contain her excitement. "You know what that means!"

Monsieur Hébert began a fantastic tale of people who could ride through the air on a log at unbelievable speeds. It was a "tall tale" if ever she heard one, but François' father told the story as though he himself had been there, and the wide-eyed children hung on his every word. With his animated voice and dramatic gestures, even the adults were mesmerized by his telling of the familiar story.

As the story came to an end Papa walked in the door with François. They were both smiling, which Anne interpreted as a good sign. She grabbed Sarah's hand and squeezed it tightly then slipped around the crowd of children to meet François. Since the others were preparing to leave, Sarah gathered up the last of the cider mugs on the table and helped put the furniture back in place.

"Sarah, you can sleep with Anne and Jeanne," Maman announced after the Héberts left. "You're no fatter than a blade of grass. There will be lots of room."

Sarah felt a sudden wave of panic. She should have left for the dyke hours ago, but the summer sun had set and she wasn't thrilled about venturing to the dyke alone. She decided to leave at first hint of dawn before the others were up.

"Hurry," Anne whispered. "I have so much to tell you." Sarah followed her new friend up the narrow stairs beside the fireplace to the small loft.

A curtain divided the girls' side of the room from Mathieu and Jean-Paul's side, which didn't afford much privacy.

"He did it," Anne exclaimed the moment they got into the room. "François asked Papa if he could marry me."

"And?" Sarah asked, already knowing what the answer would be.

"And Papa said that he would be proud to have a son from such a good family. We are going to get married this summer as soon as Father Landry arrives."

"Aren't you nervous?"

"It will be wonderful. We'll build our own house, and I'll have my own little garden. What's to be nervous about?"

"What if he's not the right one?"

"Of course he's the right one. He's my best friend. We've been best friends since we were little. Who else would I marry?"

"Stop talking about François," Jeanne whined. "I'm try-ing to sleep. You're always talking about François!" Sarah and Anne giggled as the little girl flopped down and promptly fell asleep.

"We better get some sleep or Maman will be angry," Anne warned as the two girls slid under the rough linen sheet.

Squashed between the sisters on a lumpy straw mattress in the stifling attic, Sarah considered all that had happened to her. It was totally mind-boggling, and she had no idea how it had happened. Worse, she had no idea how to reverse it. What if she couldn't get back? What if she were stuck in L'Acadie?

Chapter 9

With a start Sarah opened her eyes and spied the rough beams of the sharply angled ceiling overhead. Where was she? Not in Maggie's spare room with the sun pouring through the window. Jeanne popped into the room and bounced on the bed beside her.

"Maman said you might go back to heaven. But I'm happy you're still here."

Sarah smiled. Life was a lot less complicated for a seven-year-old.

"Ah, so you're finally up, lazybones!" Anne teased, poking her head into the loft. "I've already milked the goats and fed the pigs and chickens, but don't worry, I saved some jobs for you."

"I can't believe I slept in. I need to —— "

"Look!" Anne held out a full-length grey skirt and a white blouse as she stepped into the room. "I think Maman was up all night. They're for you."

Sarah stared, speechless. Madame LeBlanc had made clothes for her?

"Do you like them? Try them on. Maman has been so anxious for you to wake up." Anne handed the new garments to Sarah.

"These don't look like they were made from rags," Sarah commented.

"No, Maman was saving this material to make herself a skirt for my wedding. What's wrong? Don't you like them?"

Sarah blinked back tears. "They're beautiful, Anne." Sarah ran her fingers over the tiny hand-sewn stitches. "Your mother stayed up all night to make me these beautiful clothes — clothes that should have been hers."

"That's Maman for you, eh?" Anne shrugged. "Now put them on and be quick. I haven't had breakfast yet. Maman said I had to wait for you. Hurry up!"

Sarah sighed and put on the simple clothes that had so much love sewn into them. The enormity of this act of kindness overwhelmed her. They hardly even knew her.

"I can't stay," Sarah said, her eyes moist. "You understand, don't you?"

"Of course you must go." Anne smiled although Sarah could see a shadow of sadness cross her face. "Maybe you'll come back to see us. I know. You'll come for my wedding."

"I'd like that," Sarah murmured.

After breakfast, Sarah's emotions continued to roller-coaster as she walked with Anne to the dyke. She had worn her jeans under her new Acadian clothes so that she could change at the last moment. Now she handed the Acadian outfit to Anne. As much as she wanted them as a reminder of her new friends, she knew it was best to leave the clothes behind. Madame LeBlanc would be able to make good use of the new fabric.

With Anne watching from a little distance, Sarah paced back and forth on top of the dyke and wished herself back in the twenty-first century. A couple of kids raced past her playing tag. They turned and stared at her odd clothes then continued their game. But no whirlwind whisked her away. In fact, there was no wind at all. Her stomach contracted into a tight ball. She sat on the dyke hugging her knees to her chest and sobbed.

Thin arms wrapped around her shoulders. "You'll be all right," Anne whispered gently. "We'll figure it out."

Sarah dabbed her eyes. "I should have known it would be more complicated."

They both sat on the top of the dyke wondering what to do next. Finally Anne spoke.

"Maybe it's the wrong day or the wrong time. We'll try again tomorrow." Anne stood to leave.

Sarah didn't want to leave the dyke, but what else could she do? She had no idea how or why she had travelled through the centuries. If only she could wake up and find herself on Maggie's saggy sofa-bed. Reluctantly Sarah switched into her Acadian clothes in the woods. It was going to be a very long day.

Each day brought the same disappointment. Sarah tried visiting the dyke at various times of day as Anne had suggested. She had even tried wishing on a full moon. In a dark corner of her mind, a voice whispered, "What if there is no way back?" but she refused to acknowledge it. There had to be something she had overlooked.

Some two weeks later, on a bright sunny morning, Sarah carefully lifted the yoke that held the two full water buckets to her thin shoulders. Her muscles ached but she was proud of herself. She was considerably stronger than when she had arrived and now she could carry the water buckets without Anne's help. Sarah sighed as she inched toward the cottage, balancing her weighty load. Maggie's place seemed like a day at the beach in comparison. In Acadia the women seemed to do all the work. In addition to the usual cooking, hauling water, washing clothes and washing dishes, there was a myriad of other chores. Feeding the pigs, goats and chickens, tending the fields and the gardens, making cloth, sewing clothes and even replacing the straw in the mattresses and the feathers in the pillows, all fell to the women. Just when she was ready to drop from exhaustion there was one more job to do. Picking berries was the one fun job, but then there were pies and tarts to make. They also dried some berries for the winter. How Anne could be so cheerful all the time was beyond Sarah. Not that Madame LeBlanc expected her to work. Still, she could hardly sit and look at the scenery while Anne and her mother worked themselves to the bone.

Every night she longed to soak her aching muscles, but baths, to Sarah's horror, happened only once a month. That night after bringing the cows in from the field, Anne blew through the door in her usual flurry. "I have a surprise for you, my friend. Tomorrow we are going to meet Marie, my Mi'kmaq friend. She's going to teach us how to make beautiful quill boxes."

"Quill boxes?" Sarah perked up. "I lost my grandfather's special quill box when that huge wind knocked me into this century. Maybe I can make one to replace it, if I ever get back there, that is."

"Of course you'll get back," Anne said patiently, but Sarah could tell Anne no longer believed she was going anywhere.

The next morning as they walked through the woods toward the meadow, Anne chattered non-stop about plans for her wedding and her new home. Soon all the men of the village would start clearing the land for Anne and François' cottage. Sarah tried to be happy for Anne. She wanted everything to turn out well for them. But according to the movie she had seen at the interpretive centre, there would be no "happily ever after." A sense of foreboding hung over her like a heavy cloud.

Colourful wildflowers and monarch butterflies gave a magical feel to the meadow, which was alive with the sounds of cheeping chickadees and screaming jays. In the distance they saw a girl of about Anne's age. She waved.

"That's Marie," Anne said. The Mi'kmaq girl was taller and bigger boned than the petite Anne but not as tall as Sarah. Her long dark hair swished along the bottom of her linen shift as she walked towards them.

"*Kwe! Medawelein*," Anne greeted her friend in the Mi'kmaq custom.

"*Kwe* Anne," Marie replied, eyeing Sarah shyly.

Anne introduced her friends. Sarah was relieved to find out that Marie spoke French so that she could join in on the conversation. She found out that Marie's father was the chief of the nearby Mi'kmaq band and that she had two older brothers. After a short visit, they got down to the task of making the quill boxes. Marie showed them how to select the right birch tree for bark. It had to be just the right thickness. Sarah couldn't believe that they were actually going to make the delicate boxes from scratch. For some reason she had thought that they were merely decorating the boxes with the colourful quills.

The girls carefully peeled off the right amount of bark so that it wouldn't kill the tree. Then they used an awl-like tool for etching the design on the bark. According to Marie, the design was for the top of the box. Black spruce root was wrapped in a vertical pattern to make the sides. Sarah couldn't quite picture her little hunk of bark looking like her grandparents' beautiful container. There was obviously a lot more work to be done. They still needed quills, which weren't even dyed yet.

"Come with me." Marie motioned with her hand. "I will show you Grandmother's quill boxes. She makes the most beautiful ones." She smiled warmly at Sarah. "That way you will be encouraged and want to finish yours."

Anne looked up at the position of the sun. It was already high overhead. "We will have to be quick. Maman will be looking for us soon."

The girls walked for several minutes through thick bushes, picking berries to munch as they went. To Sarah it seemed as if they would never get there. She wasn't impressed with all the scrapes and scratches she was getting from overhanging branches. Finally the forest opened up into a large clearing sprinkled with wigwams. The wigwams were birch structures rather than the hide tipis she had seen in museums. A group of children were sitting around a wooden bowl with little bone dice inside it. They stopped their game and stared as the girls walked by. Marie spoke sharply to them and they quickly looked down and continued playing.

"What are they doing?" Sarah asked. "It looks very interesting."

"It's a game called waltes," Anne told her. "Points are given depending on how the dice roll — which side turns up."

Sarah had never seen circular dice like these made out of bone. Marie disappeared into one of the wigwams. When she came out she was carrying two ornate containers. She displayed them proudly for her friends to see.

Sarah gasped. The box in Marie's right hand could have been her grandfather's.

Marie noticed her staring at the little box and handed it to her. "Grandmother finished this one just this morning."

Sarah studied the familiar blue diamond flower pattern on the top. From the blue petals of the flower, which were outlined in red and green, to the zigzag pattern on the side, the entire quill box looked identical.

"This must be a popular pattern," Sarah said to Anne showing her the quill box. "It's exactly like the one I lost on the dyke."

Anne's words bubbled out as she excitedly explained to Marie about the quill box Sarah lost.

"Then it is yours," Marie said softly.

"But it belongs to your grandmother," Sarah insisted. "I shouldn't take it just because it's the same as the one I lost."

"I will go and ask her about it." Marie disappeared again into the wigwam but was not gone for long. "Grandmother says she made it for you." Marie handed the beautiful treasure back to Sarah.

It was an odd thing to say, Sarah thought, but generous and thoughtful. Now she would be able to replace the one she lost. Anne chattered all the way back to the LeBlanc cottage but Sarah said barely a word. A comforting warmth washed over her. She thought about the day on the dyke when she was holding the quill box. She had been studying the colours and the pattern, which was why she was so sure that this one from Marie looked the same. When she had opened the lid to put in the stone, that's when the wind almost whisked her off the dyke. "That's it!" Sarah said out loud.

"What? What are you talking about? You haven't even been listening to me, have you?"

"When I opened the lid to the quill box, that's when the wind came and brought me here."

"And then the box disappeared back to its home," Anne said excitedly.

"What do you mean?"

"Marie said that her grandmother had just finished making the quill box this morning."

Confused, Sarah looked at Anne for a minute and then she understood what her friend was getting at. Could it be that the little box disappeared because it hadn't been made yet? Was it possible that this *was* the very same quill box that she lost? "I haven't been able to go back because I needed the quill box," Sarah said thoughtfully. She could hardly wait to get to the dyke. She had the feeling that it was time to go home.

Chapter 10

Sarah stood on the dyke with Anne and wondered if the winds of L'Acadie would take her home now. "I'll miss you, Anne. Tell your family that I'll think of them often."

"We'll miss you too," Anne replied. "I've never had an angel for a sister before."

"Don't start on that again!" They laughed and hugged.

Sarah wanted to tell Anne about the dark days ahead, to warn her so she could prepare in some way. She wanted to say that she was sorry for what Anne and her family would go through. Her heart was full of so many things, but words escaped her.

Maybe the quill box wouldn't even work. It seemed like a

silly idea to her now. She began to feel light-headed as though she might faint. After giving Anne one final hug, she carefully lifted the lid. The wind swept her into its grip immediately.

"Saraaah!" Anne's voice echoed on the waves of the wind as Sarah catapulted into the black oblivion. Gradually Anne's voice and the roaring wind faded into the distance.

Sarah opened her eyes, still dizzy and shaken by the wind. The air held a damp chill and Anne was nowhere in sight. In the distance she could see Luke coming towards her across the open field. Incredible relief and incredible sadness flowed through her veins.

"Enjoying the view?" Luke asked as he approached the dyke.

"I guess." What a strange comment after she'd been gone for two weeks.

"Did you go for a walk along the dyke?"

"The dyke's not *that* long," Sarah answered, still perplexed by his comments.

"What are you talking about?"

"What am I talking about? You're the one who's acting as though nothing has happened."

"Man, being cooped up all day in the attic must have clogged your brain cells!"

"The attic?" Sarah couldn't make sense of this whole conversation.

"That was you up there in the attic cleaning out Maggie's junk this afternoon, wasn't it?"

"*That* was today?" Sarah pronounced each word slowly as she sank down to the ground. It was wet and mucky but she barely noticed.

Luke knelt down beside her, a bewildered look on his face. "Did you hit your head again or something, Sarah?" he asked gently.

"No, I did not hit my head." Sarah felt tired, too tired to try to figure out Luke's response to her absence.

"Come on, Sarah." Luke offered his hand to her. "You're getting all wet. Let's go home."

Home? Sarah didn't even know the meaning of the word any more. She reached for his hand. It felt warm and reassuring. Luke had said *this afternoon* when he mentioned the attic. Was that possible?

"What's the date today?" Sarah asked as they walked toward Maggie's.

"July 16th, all day. Why?"

"I couldn't remember, that's all," Sarah mumbled. It was the same day. No time had lapsed during her stay with the LeBlanc family. It was all too much to think about.

Maggie was no more surprised to see her than Luke had been. She also assumed that she had been out on the dyke only for a few minutes.

Sarah took comfort in the overstuffed chair and sipped the hot cocoa Maggie had made. She stared at the fire, her mind filled with memories of another stone fireplace in another time. Maybe it was all a dream after all — a very weird, very realistic dream. Or maybe she *had* bumped her head and been knocked unconscious again as Luke suggested. She noticed Luke and Maggie exchange worried glances when she gave one-word answers to their questions.

Maggie perched on the chubby arm of the chair and grasped Sarah's hand.

"Good grief, Luke. What did you guys do up there in the attic? Scrub all the junk with boiling bleach? Look at Sarah's hands. They're practically raw."

"Yeah, that's it. We scrubbed all the junk before we put it in the trash bag, Aunt Maggie." Luke turned to Sarah. "I thought you wore gloves."

Sarah nodded staring at her rough callused hands as though they belonged to someone else. Her arms were firmer too, not so soft looking. No, it hadn't been a dream. Maggie and Luke exchanged looks again, but neither of them made further mention of her hands or the attic.

Sarah finished the hot chocolate and made her way upstairs. She was relieved to be away from everyone. Exhausted, she was asleep the moment her head hit the pillow.

─❦─

"I'm telling you, Maggie. It's weird. Something happened to Sarah on the dyke." Luke leaned on his knuckles at the table, trying to make sense of the evening's events.

"She did seem to be acting a little odd," Maggie commented. "But she's gone through a lot lately, don't forget."

"I know, but Maggie, she didn't even know what day it was and she was angry that I didn't ask where she had been. It was as though she thought she had been gone for a long time. And what about her hands? All she did in the attic was dust a few things and shuffle a few things around; she definitely didn't do anything that would have roughed up her hands like that. Now that I think about it, she was acting kind of strange then, too."

Maggie looked thoughtful as though she were about to say something and then changed her mind. "These old bones are ready for bed, kiddo. It's been a long day and six A.M. will come soon enough. Maybe things will look different in the morning."

Luke wasn't so sure about that, but Aunt Maggie did look beat and he didn't want to trouble her anymore. "I'm sure you're right. Good night, Aunt Maggie."

"Good night, Luke." Maggie rinsed her mug then started toward the stairs. She turned back for a moment. "And don't worry too much about Sarah, Luke. She'll be all right."

"Whatever you say, boss!" Luke grinned, attempting to hide his worry. He tossed and turned all night replaying the conversation with Sarah over and over in his mind. What could she possibly have been talking about? This was not the same Sarah that he had met in the market or the Sarah he had spent the day with on the boat. Tonight her face was more serious, older somehow, and her hands were rough and callused. Down in the depths of his belly a fear twisted his insides into knots. Had Sarah's head been more affected than anyone realized from the concussion she suffered the day of the storm? Was her brain short-circuiting now? He had heard of that sort of thing. It still didn't explain what had happened to her hands, but somehow he suspected there was a connection.

Luke was still awake when the birds announced dawn. He had dozed off and on, but sleep, for the most part, had eluded him. He gave his head a shake. A cold shower and a mug of Maggie's brew should do the trick, he thought as he dragged himself out of bed.

All through breakfast Luke thought about how to convince Maggie that he should stick around home for the day. Sarah was still sleeping, but when she got up he didn't want her to be left alone. Not until he knew if she were all right. He tried some subtle hints about repairs that needed to be done around the place but Aunt Maggie wasn't biting. He'd have to out-and-out ask if he could take the day off. He dreaded that. Of course she'd want to know why. The phone rang just as Luke was about to risk the direct approach.

"Well, you're off the hook, good-lookin'!" Aunt Maggie said, grinning like the Cheshire cat as she hung up the phone. "Pete White is getting out of hospital today. I told Reta you'd drive Sarah into Halifax to pick them up this afternoon. I have a feeling you won't be protesting too much this time about taking Sarah for a drive." Aunt Maggie chuckled, apparently pleased with herself.

"You needn't look so smug," Luke answered, amazed that Maggie could read him so well. "No one's given you a crystal ball yet."

"Ha! Who needs a crystal ball with the delightful Miss White around?"

Luke could feel himself turning several shades of red.

"Since you're not coming in to work today, you can fix Sarah's breakfast for her. Invite everyone here for supper too, will you? They won't have a chance to get groceries or anything."

"Yes ma'am. Anything you say." Luke brought his right hand up in mock salute.

Sarah came down for breakfast a few minutes later.

"I've made some pancakes and bacon for breakfast if you're hungry," Luke offered.

"Thanks."

"We got good news this morning," Luke said, attempting to carry on a normal conversation. "Your grandfather is getting out of the hospital today."

"That's good. I'm glad he's finally better. It seems like ages since I've seen him." Sarah sat at the large table while Luke filled her plate with hot apple pancakes.

"I'll be driving into Halifax to pick up your grandparents this afternoon. Want to come? They'll be more anxious to see you than me."

"Yes, I'd like that." Sarah picked at her food and stared out the window.

"So are you going to tell me about it?" Luke asked as they sped along the highway.

"About what?" Sarah fidgeted nervously, clenching and unclenching her hands.

"You're right. It's none of my business." Luke fell silent. He couldn't say that he blamed her. Why should she trust him? He was probably the cause of her problems in the first place. For the millionth time since that freaky storm, Luke regretted taking Sarah sailing that day.

"You wouldn't believe me," she practically whispered the words.

"Try me." Luke gripped the steering wheel, watching her reactions out of the corner of his eye.

"There are some things that can be explained and other things that just happen. Things you can't explain."

"For example?" Luke probed.

Sarah drew in a deep breath and expelled it slowly as though she were preparing for a painful event. "Do you remember mentioning that I was speaking French in my sleep after hitting my head?"

Luke nodded. Here it comes. He knew it had something to do with that wretched boat trip.

"I didn't mention it to you, but when I got knocked out on the boat that day, I saw this strange vision of an Acadian girl."

"Vision?"

"Well, kind of like a dream. Anyway, it was the same girl that was on the dyke that day that we cleaned out the attic," Sarah continued.

"Yesterday, you mean? How could the girl from your dream be on the dyke? That makes no sense."

"Her name is Anne and I just spent two weeks living with her family in 1755." Sarah blurted the words out as though once started there was no stopping them.

"Whoa, slow down." Luke pulled into a roadside turnout and looked over at Sarah. This was more serious than he thought. "We cleaned out the attic yesterday, Sarah."

Sarah's brow wrinkled as she continued, "I was stuck there for a while because I didn't know how to get back. When I finally got back here, no time had passed. That's the really weird part."

That's not the only weird part, Luke thought, but he kept his mouth shut.

"I don't expect you to believe me," Sarah said as if reading his mind, "but if I don't tell someone I'm going to burst. So I'll start at the beginning, then you'll declare me certifiable and we'll both go back to living normal lives."

"Go for it." At least she had a sense of humour about it. She couldn't be that far gone. And she couldn't be serious about this 1755 thing. There had to be a catch.

"After we finished in the attic," Sarah began, "I went back to my room. I couldn't get that Acadian girl from the dyke out of my mind. I was looking at the quill box I had brought from my grandparents' house when I decided to go for a walk. Now that I think about it, I felt drawn to the dyke, as though I expected the girl to be there or something. Anyway, I still had the quill box in my hand when I reached the dyke. There was a pretty stone that I found so I took the lid off the quill box to put the stone inside. That's when this crazy wind took hold of me. It was really wild. There was a loud roar and everything went black. I thought I was in the centre of a whirlwind or something. Next thing I knew, I was staring into the face of the Acadian girl and it was 1755."

A troubled feeling spread through Luke's body as Sarah proceeded to tell a fantastic story about life in eighteenth-century Acadia. She actually believed that she had been there in the eighteenth century, that she had really hauled water to the house, washed clothes by hand and plucked chickens to make pies. He knew that she might have had more damage from the concussion than anyone had realized, but he had no idea that it was this bad. Sarah stopped talking and closed her eyes. She looked drained, as though the story had totally zapped her energy. Luke drove in silence for the next few minutes. What a wild story.

"Promise me that you won't tell Maggie or my grandparents, Luke," Sarah said finally. "It'll just worry them. They have enough on their minds right now."

Yeah, like he would go telling people this insane story.

"Luke, do you promise?" Sarah sounded panicky.

Sarah's eyes had that frightened, trapped animal look in them, which increased his already uneasy feeling.

"Sure, I promise. I won't tell anyone." Man, was she acting like a nutcase!

"Good." Sarah closed her eyes again and the lines in her face relaxed.

It was best to just let her sleep, Luke thought. They would pick up her grandparents and then he'd see how things went. Once she got settled back at her grandparents' house, maybe she would gradually come back to normal on her own. He sure hoped so.

Chapter 11

"Yer going to scrub the roses clear off that tea pot," Sarah's grandfather remarked one afternoon. "We'll have to start callin' you Cinderella."

Sarah smiled at how protective her grandfather was. "If it'll make you feel better I'll get my book and enjoy your new deck."

"Now there's a good idea."

Sarah finished the lunch dishes and ran upstairs to get a book. She was halfway down the stairs after retrieving *The Acadian Exiles* book she had borrowed from Maggie, when she overheard her grandparents talking.

"She needs to get out and have some fun with kids her

own age, not play nursemaid to an old man and work her fingers to the bone."

Her grandmother sighed. "Well, it has been nice having a hardworking young person about the house. How she learned to work that way, being brought up with maids and servants galore, is beyond me. I guess we must have taught Nicole something to have such an industrious granddaughter."

Sarah almost laughed out loud at that comment. She had never lifted a finger until that day in Maggie's attic, but it had been her stay at Anne's that had taught her what real work was. She had to admit that washing dishes by hand with hot running water from a tap didn't seem so tough any more.

"She doesn't seem to mind puttering around the house," her grandmother was saying. "I haven't heard any complaints."

"She's too polite to complain," her grandfather commented. "Wish I could take her out sightseeing or something."

"Stop your worrying, we'll think of something. Meanwhile I'm going to get out that box of old photographs and start organizing them into albums. Maybe we'll find some that Sarah would like to keep."

Her grandfather was in the kitchen busily gluing together little blue and white pieces of ceramic when Sarah walked through on her way to the deck.

"Do you need me to get you anything before I hit the deck?" she asked.

"Not a thing. You go and relax. I'll probably join you in a few minutes. I'll just finish gluing this little ceramic magnet for Reta. A friend brought it back from Holland for her. This little windmill was her favourite fridge magnet, before someone slammed the door too hard and it popped off and broke."

"I'm sure that person didn't mean to slam the door too hard." Sarah grinned at her grandfather as though they shared a big secret. The screen door clacked closed behind her as she settled herself into a large wooden deck chair. She opened to the chapter called "The Lawrence Regime." She wanted to understand the Acadian situation better . . . not that she could do anything about it. Sarah sighed and began to read. But the more she read, the more frustrated she became. It was all so unfair. Both France and England wanted Acadia only as a weapon or a means of gaining control. France was happy for the Acadians "to be a thorn in Great Britain's side," but at the same time England didn't really want them to leave. Great Britain had actually made concessions to try to keep the Acadians. "How odd," Sarah muttered to herself.

Her grandfather hobbled out on his crutches and carefully lowered himself into the chair beside her. He glanced at the worn book in her lap. "Reta and I were just saying this morning that you need to get out and do something other than scrubbing pots and reading dusty old history books. You haven't had much of a vacation yet, what with one accident or another."

"Stuff happens," Sarah answered. "It's not your fault."

"It isn't a matter of fault, and I know you wouldn't complain, but you do look a little down in the mouth right now."

"Reading about the Acadians frustrates me." Sarah held up the faded volume. "I'm trying to figure out why the deportation took place but it's very confusing. I thought that the Acadians were deported because they refused to sign the Oath of Allegiance to England, but according to this book England actually prevented the Acadians from leaving."

"Yes, I believe I've read something about that," her grandfather answered thoughtfully.

"Apparently, just before Governor Lawrence came on the scene, England actually made concessions to get the Acadians to stay. Why would that be?"

"Power," her grandfather stated simply. "It always comes down to power and control, and the egos of the people who want power and control. It caused problems in the eighteenth century, and it's still causing us problems today."

"But how was keeping the Acadians in Nova Scotia giving England power? I thought they wanted to be rid of the Acadians. Weren't they a threat?"

"It is a complicated story, my dear. You have to understand that this fight was not about a bit of land around the

Minas Basin, although it was prime farm land. This fight was about control of North America. France was quite happy to let Acadia irritate England, but England, well England hated to let the Acadians slide over to the side of the enemy."

"What do you mean? I thought they were the enemy?" Sarah gave her head a shake. This was not making sense.

"Yes and no. The Acadians had been pretty much ignored by France, so they didn't feel a particularly strong allegiance either way. They were a peace-loving people. They signed a conditional oath, which stated that in the case of war they would not take up arms against the English. If England could appease the Acadians, turn a blind eye to their not signing an unconditional oath of allegiance, then at least they wouldn't fight against England on the side of France."

"I guess that makes sense," Sarah said thoughtfully. "Obviously things changed when Governor Lawrence took over."

"Yes," her grandfather agreed. "Governor Lawrence thought it was just a matter of time before the Acadians caused serious problems for them. The Acadians already outnumbered the English in Nova Scotia significantly." Her grandfather paused. "I guess he didn't believe that they would stay neutral forever."

"Good grief, have you two not got anything more interesting to talk about than some political problem that happened 250 years ago?" Reta brought out a tray of cookies and lemonade and set them on a little glass patio table. "Perhaps these snacks will take your mind off of it."

"It *is* interesting," Sarah said. "Especially since there are still issues between the English and French today. We are supposed to be a bilingual country but I think New Brunswick is the only officially bilingual province. Maybe I'll do some research on the Acadians while I'm here and use it for a school project."

"Homework in the summer? You must have a screw loose!" Pete White laughed.

"For heaven's sake, Pete," Reta interjected. "Some people like to challenge themselves. There's nothing wrong with that. Good grief, you'd think being a hard worker was a crime or something. Anyways, you two carry on with your political talk if you want. I'm going to get back to organizing those pictures."

"Would you like some help?" Sarah offered. She was eager to see the pictures.

"That would be lovely. But you sit there and have your lemonade first while I get the photos into the right piles. Then we can work on putting them in the new album. The old one just plum fell apart."

"You need to get out and see the sights and do something," her grandfather said after Reta went back inside. "You could go into Halifax and go shopping or go to the natural history museum or the harbour. There's lots of history in Halifax if it's history that turns your crank. Why don't you ask Luke if he would take you into the city? I'm sure he wouldn't mind."

As if on cue, Luke let himself in the back gate.

"Were your ears burnin'?" Pete White asked as Luke joined them on the deck. "We were just talking about you."

"You must be pretty hard up for conversation," Luke joked. He pulled up a chair next to Sarah's grandfather. "So have you been taking it easy and behaving yourself?"

"As a matter of fact, I'm enjoying the charming company of my beautiful granddaughter. I tell you, Luke, if I'd known the kind of service I was going to get I woulda taken a tumble long ago!" Pete White chuckled. "I was just mentioning to Nurse Nightingale here that she should take a break from her gruelling duties and go into Halifax or something. Think you'd be interested in taking a pretty girl to Halifax for a day?"

"I can take the bus," Sarah added quickly. She didn't want Luke to think he was stuck with her again.

"Let's go to that little coffee shop on Main Street for an iced cappuccino, and talk about a trip into Halifax," Luke suggested. He turned to Pete. "If you can spare Sarah for a while, that is."

"Good plan!" her grandfather said. "She's become a bit of a workaholic these days. Now she's even planning a school project about the Acadians."

"Maybe I can straighten out her priorities."

Sarah shot Luke a piercing glare. "I told my grandmother I'd help her put photographs in albums."

"You two take off." Pete White waved his hands dismissing them. "And take your time. The pictures will still be here when you get back."

-ℓℓ-

The little café was crowded and noisy but Sarah decided it was a nice change of scenery. They took their iced cappuccinos to a table on the patio where they could catch some afternoon sun.

"Hey Luke! How's it going?" A tall, skinny guy with spiky blond hair approached the table.

"Can't complain," Luke shrugged. "Tim, I'd like you to meet Sarah. She's visiting here for the summer from Toronto."

"Spending the summer slumming, are ya?" Tim laughed loudly. "Maybe I should spend some time in the big city. I didn't know what I was missing before now." He nudged Luke and gave him a thumbs-up.

"Tim!" A chunky redhead with a tight black Harley Davidson t-shirt yelled from the parking lot. "Get your butt in gear. We're gonna be late!"

"Gotta go, the master calls." Tim slapped Luke on the back. "Later!"

"Saved by the redhead," Luke said, grinning. "Tim's a little hard to take at times but he's harmless. By the way, sorry if I didn't exactly ask if you wanted to go for a coffee." Luke looked down at his hands. "I guess I didn't want to give you the option of saying no."

"No problem. I could have said no." Sarah sipped her cool drink, surprised at the apology.

"You've probably had more than your share of people planning your life for you, as it is."

Sarah looked at him in amazement. "How did you guess?"

"For starters, I don't think it was your idea to hang out with me that day you came to Maggie's. Secondly, I'm guessing Wolfville was not your idea of a vacation destination."

Sarah laughed. "You got that right! But it's not as bad as I thought it was going to be."

"That's good to hear."

They chatted easily about Maggie and the goings on at the market and about *Sweet Betsy*. But Sarah couldn't get the LeBlanc family out of her mind. The more she thought about it, the more convinced she was that she had to make one more trip to the past.

"Where do you go?" Luke asked out of the blue.

"What do you mean?"

"Sometimes you go all quiet and you get this strange look on your face. I can tell your mind is far away."

Sarah blushed. "I guess I've spent too many hours on my own. I'm not very good company."

"That's not what I meant. I just wondered what you were thinking about."

Sarah thought about it for a moment. Should she tell Luke the truth? He would think she was crazy, but then he already thought she was crazy.

"I need to get more information on the deportation," she began. For the first time she looked Luke straight in the eye, wondering if she had the courage to say what was on her mind.

"Oh yeah, the school project."

"It's not exactly a school project," Sarah paused clenching her hands together. "I have to go back."

Luke eyed her suspiciously. "Please tell me you're talking about going back to your grandparents' house."

Sarah shook her head. "To help Anne." It was almost a whisper. "I need to warn the LeBlancs about the deportation."

Luke held his head in his hands.

"I know what you're thinking, Luke," Sarah said, her voice serious. "You think I scrambled my brain when I hit my head. You think I've lost touch with reality."

"The thought has crossed my mind," Luke admitted.

"Sometimes I feel that way myself. That it couldn't have happened. But it did. I could tell you stuff you won't find in any history book."

"You're serious about this, aren't you?"

Sarah held her hands up for Luke to see. "I didn't get these calluses from a dream or an overactive imagination."

"Okay. Let's say that you did go back in time — that you can go back in time — what good would that do? You can't change history, Sarah. The deportation happened, period. There's nothing you can do to change that." He finished his coffee, frustration written on his furrowed forehead.

"You don't get it, do you?" Sarah accused. "Before, the Acadians were just a sad story in a book, but now they're real people that I lived with and worked alongside. I saved Jean-Paul's life, and for what? So they could all be packed away on boats and maybe never even see each other again!" Sarah realized that as the passion in her voice grew so did the decibels, and people were staring. Luke, to his credit, never took his eyes off her. If he was embarrassed by her passionate outburst, he didn't show it. He sat quietly for a moment before speaking.

"You didn't say anything about saving anyone's life before. How did that happen?"

"It's a long story. I'll tell you about it sometime."

"How about on the way into Halifax?"

"You sound like my grandfather now. Everyone's trying to get me out doing something. You all think I've lost it."

"Well, maybe we can kill two birds with one stone."

"Meaning?"

"Meaning, Halifax has the Public Archives of Nova Scotia. You could look up information about the deportation. Maybe find out where Anne's family ended up, and your grandparents will be happy that you're out sightseeing."

"Really? Do you think they'll have Acadian genealogies?"

"Yeah, they have lots of information on the Acadian history and genealogies. I checked it out once myself."

"You did? Are you Acadian?" Sarah thought again about the name Hébert. Was it more than a coincidence that Maggie's last name was also Hébert?

"My mother's family is Acadian."

"That's why you know so much about the deportation."

"I've read up on it some. But to be honest with you, I never got far in my search for my mother's family. I lost patience."

"So you don't mind taking me to the archives in Halifax?"

"All those musty old books in a dark, dingy basement, away from the glare of the hot summer sun? I wouldn't miss it for anything."

"When could we go?"

"How about Monday? It's our slowest day and Maggie doesn't mind holding the fort on her own."

"Monday would be perfect." She knew that Luke still didn't believe her story but she didn't care.

Chapter 12

Luke picked Sarah up promptly at nine on Monday morning. "I brought you something," he said as she eased into the jeep. He handed her a fat brown envelope. Sarah curiously slid out the stacks of pages obviously printed off the Internet. There were biographies of Governor Lawrence, and of Colonel Winslow, who carried out the drastic orders. Sarah flipped through the pages. There was a list of all the transport ships, where they departed from, and their destination points. There was even information on how to search the genealogies at the archives and lists of books on Acadian history.

"I'm impressed. When did you find all this?"

"On the weekend. It's amazing what you can 'Google.' I know how overwhelming the archives can be so I thought this might help you. Did you see the list of books on the Acadians? It might be easier to ask for a few resources by name."

"Thanks. This must have taken you a while." Sarah was sincerely touched by his thoughtfulness.

"I hope it's helpful."

"I'm sure it will be. I didn't even think of searching the Internet." Sarah continued to peruse the various articles.

"Considering your grandparents don't own a computer, I'm not surprised."

"I was thinking of checking out the library at Acadia University. It would have some information, wouldn't it?"

"It does, but the archives will be better for the kind of specific information you want."

The drive took a little over an hour and Sarah was surprised at how quickly the time passed. She found out a bit more about Luke's family in Halifax and even talked a bit about her mother's television show. She also managed to skim through some of the information from Luke. It was amazing how many articles on the deportation there were.

When they arrived at the archives the registration staff instructed them to deposit all their personal belongings in a locker. Sarah grabbed her pen and pad of paper out of her backpack and followed Luke to the third floor reference section. An elderly gentleman, who introduced himself as

Mr. Wiggley, showed them around. He explained how to access the information they might be looking for. He also pointed out a map on a large poster depicting how many Acadians were deported from each location and the various places they were deported to. Sarah made a mental note to go back to that after he finished showing them around. By the time Mr. Wiggley was finished, he had pulled a stack of books and documents he thought they might be interested in and settled them into a reading room.

"Well, let's get started." Sarah sat behind the overwhelming pile, her head spinning. She decided to start with the transport ships that had left Grand-Pré. If she could find out where the families landed, perhaps she could find out what happened to Anne's family. Maybe there were lists of passengers so she could find out which colony they had arrived at. That, at least, would narrow the search. Sarah looked up every chapter that dealt specifically with the deportation events, including the pages Luke had printed off, frantically recording any information she thought might be pertinent. So far she hadn't found any passenger lists but she did learn the names of the five ships that were filled with families from Grand-Pré. Each ship appeared to have gone to a different place. Finding one family was not very likely — not in the time she had.

"Hey, look at this, Sarah." Luke held out the book so she could read it. "It's a letter from Governor Lawrence written to Colonel Winslow in Grand-Pré."

Sarah's stomach churned as she read the heartless orders to get rid of all of the Acadians at any cost. He even suggested that the men be shipped off without the women and children if need be.

"What a loser," Luke commented.

"That's an understatement." Sarah sighed. "I'm going to look at that map of the deportation that's on the wall." Maybe that will spark a brainwave, she thought. She wasn't sure what she was looking for anymore.

Sarah studied the large yellow arrows on the map indicating the routes the various transports had taken. There was a little caption by each of the arrows recounting a brief history of Acadians at each location. The size of the arrow indicated how many Acadians had arrived there. The fattest arrow pointed to Louisiana, which had been a French colony until 1762, and so it welcomed the Acadians. In the years that followed the deportation in Grand-Pré, it became a huge focal point for Acadian migration and the Cajun culture was born. Unfortunately none of the Acadians from 1755 were deported to Louisiana, Sarah noticed. Still, Anne's family could have migrated there later. Well, she was right about one thing. Searching for a specific family was pointless. She needed to be proactive. There had to be something she could find out that would help Anne's family if she were able to go back in time once more. Sarah wandered back to the reading room deep in thought about what she could do. Looking at the poster with its fat yellow arrows and reading about the horrid treatment the Acadians received convinced Sarah all the more that she had to make one more trip back in time. It was one thing for her not to know the awful events that took place. It was another entirely to know and not do anything.

Sarah delved into the stack of books, reading and rereading the various accounts of what happened in those final weeks and days leading up to the deportation. She also discovered that the Acadians had been treated cruelly by the receiving colonies. With a sense of desperation, Sarah recorded the details, as though by merely gathering all the facts, she could somehow save Anne from this fate. She found a book called *The History of Halifax*. It was an interesting change from all the depressing deportation stuff. The date 1753 caught her eye. "Listen to this, Luke. The *Halifax Gazette* was started in 1753. It was Canada's first newspaper."

"Cool." Luke closed the book he was reading. He stood up and stretched.

"It was owned by John Bushell. His daughter Elizabeth worked at the paper with him. She helped run the paper and was a presswoman."

"That's interesting." Luke stifled a yawn.

"For a woman to be a reporter and help run a paper in 1753 is pretty impressive, you have to admit."

"That's true. Any chance of getting something to eat sometime in the near future?" Luke asked. "I'm starved."

"Sure." Sarah looked bleakly at her copious notes and at the pile of books she had barely skimmed through.

"It would take weeks to go through all this stuff, Sarah. Even if we stay until closing time you'd hardly make a dent in that pile."

"I know you're right." Sarah put the lid on her pen and shoved her papers under the clip on her clipboard rather forcefully. "It was getting kind of frustrating anyway."

"Maybe we could come back again next week."

"Maybe." Sarah had no intention of waiting until next week. The sooner she made the trip to the past, the better.

Luke shrugged. It was difficult to figure out what Sarah wanted.

"I thought we'd go to Fisherman's Cove to eat," Luke said after they had signed out. "There's a nice little restaurant there with great food, overlooking the water. There are also a lot of little shops I thought you might want to look in."

"Did my grandfather have anything to do with this plan?" Sarah asked.

"Fisherman's Cove is my idea, but I have to admit that I'll be in big trouble with Pete if I don't take you to at least one tourist spot while we're in Halifax."

"Fisherman's Cove it is." Sarah wasn't overly enthusiastic but she was feeling a little hungry. Perhaps a change of scenery would be a nice break from the depressing deportation stories.

It was a short scenic drive to Fisherman's Cove, then

Luke pulled into the parking lot of a building with a bright red roof sporting giant letters that spelled *Boondocks*. The waiter seated them on the deck overlooking the water and any misgivings Sarah had about leaving the archives dissipated. She shaded her eyes from the sun glinting off the water and inhaled the salty sea breeze. Yes, the change of scenery was not such a bad idea.

Sarah and Luke both ordered the lobster. While they waited for their meals, Luke told Sarah a little about the area. Apparently it was a two-hundred-year-old restored fishing village. Today it was an authentic working fishing village but there were also lots of little shops for the tourists. *Two hundred* years old, Sarah thought. Only fifty some years after the deportation.

"I never did tell you about when I saved Jean-Paul from drowning, did I?" Sarah asked suddenly.

"No, you didn't," Luke answered less than enthusiastically.

"It was when I first got there," Sarah continued. "Jean-Paul is Anne's five-year-old brother. He had fallen into the river and swallowed a lot of water. Honestly Luke, I was so scared. I'd never used my CPR training in a real emergency before." Sarah's cheeks flushed as she got caught up in the drama of the story. "It was the first time I had done anything that made a difference — I mean a real difference," Sarah said as she finished the story. "I actually saved his life. I can't describe the feeling. It was amazing."

Sarah noticed that Luke didn't talk a lot after that. They

stopped at a few of the shops after lunch, but neither of them was really in the mood for it now. Everything reminded Sarah of Anne's family, which drove Luke crazy. It seemed impossible for her to stay in the present. The drive home was quiet. Sarah knew that Luke was upset about her talking about Anne's family again, but she couldn't help it. The details of the deportation consumed her, and she knew they would continue to do so until she did something to help her friends.

Chapter 13

Luke lay on his bed staring at the ceiling. Sarah's weird stories tumbled through his mind. He rose from his bed and paced uneasily around the room. She definitely needed help. They both needed help! She was turning him into a nutcase with all this nonsense. Luke pounded his fist into the bedroom door so hard that his knuckles stung.

"Hey! What's with the demolition derby?" Maggie shouted from downstairs.

"Sorry Maggie, I didn't know you were home."

"So that's what you do when I'm not home? Pound the livin' daylights out of the place? Come downstairs. We need to talk."

Luke took his time, pondering what he would tell Maggie, but nothing brilliant came to mind. Maggie pointed to the plaid squashy chair by the fire and handed him a mug of steaming coffee. She got right to the point.

"So, what's up with you and Sarah?"

"I had a frustrating day, Aunt Maggie. How was your day?" Luke was used to his aunt's bluntness, but he still didn't think it would hurt for her to be a little less direct once in a while, especially when he needed to stall for time.

"Cut the nonsense. You know darn well I didn't call you down here to talk about the weather."

"Nothing is *up* between Sarah and me. I took her to Halifax, but you know that. Then I drove her home. That's it."

Maggie's sharp eyes pierced his gaze. "So, you pounding your knuckles to mush had nothing to do with Sarah?" She didn't look convinced. "You're acting mighty odd these days, Luke, and I'd say it started when Sarah arrived on the scene."

"Odd? OK, I'll tell you what's odd. Sarah is obsessed with the Acadians."

"Nothin' wrong with learnin' about history. Got some Acadian blood myself in these old veins."

"This is way beyond curiosity about the history of the area. We're talkin' obsession with a capital 'O.' She dreams about it and everything. She's . . ." Luke tried to think of what to say without actually breaking his promise. "It's not natural. I mean, there's something wrong," he finished clumsily.

Maggie's eyes narrowed to slits. "Why do I get the impression you're not telling me everything?"

Luke stared into his coffee mug. "I promised I wouldn't say anything. I've probably already said more than I should."

"I'd be the last one to tell you to break a promise. You know that." Maggie's voice was calm and even. "But if you think keeping your promise is in any way harmful to Sarah, you have the obligation to let someone know, promise or not. I won't pester you any more about it. But you need to think about that."

They both sat for a time looking into the fire. Maggie didn't push, and Luke was grateful for that.

"I just don't know what to do, Maggie." Luke tapped his fingers on the edge of his mug. "She's been behaving strangely ever since — "

"Ever since the storm when she hit her head," Maggie finished the sentence for him.

"Possibly."

"Is there something I could do?"

Luke thought for a moment. "She really respects you. Maybe you could invite her over to help you make pickles or something. I don't know if she'd talk to you about it, but it's worth a try."

"Pete's birthday is on Saturday," Maggie mused. "She could help organize a surprise party for him. He's turning seventy-five, and with all the commotion Reta hasn't had a chance to plan anything special for him."

"Aunt Maggie, you're brilliant!"

"Thanks for the vote of confidence, son." Maggie patted Luke's hand. "And now, if you think you can manage without pounding any holes in the plaster, I'm going to do some paper work before turning in."

ℓℓ

Maggie's plan went off smoothly. She invited Sarah over for a couple of days to help plan her grandfather's party. Reta was thrilled about the idea of a party, and Pete thought Sarah was helping Maggie make pickles. Luke hoped it would be the perfect opportunity for Sarah to talk to Maggie about her Acadian *experience*.

All the next day Luke, Sarah and Maggie organized the party. Sarah helped Maggie clean the entire house and make floral arrangements with flowers from Maggie's garden, while Luke delivered invitations and cut the grass. He hoped Sarah would talk to Maggie about the Acadian thing, but maybe the party had taken her mind off it. When he got back from delivering the invitations Sarah was up in the attic working on her birthday present, which he gathered was a painting — probably of her grandmother's roses.

"How's it going?" he asked as he climbed into the attic.

Sarah moved away from the easel. "It's almost finished, Luke. What do you think?"

A shiver raced along Luke's spine. This was definitely not

her grandmother's garden. There in front of him was an idyllic scene of an Acadian cottage. A short round Acadian woman stood in the doorway, her hands on her hips. Young willows lined a trail leading to the cottage, and a few scraggly goats grazed in the rough enclosure beside the thatched-roof barn. Tiny purple flowers graced the flax field beyond. The detail was breathtaking.

"Well?" Sarah prodded. "What do you think?"

Luke continued to stare at the painting. "I've never seen anything like it."

"And that would be a good thing, right?"

"Yeah." Luke nodded. "That would be a good thing." He couldn't take his eyes off it.

"Thanks. I really tried to capture the feeling of the place."

The feeling of the place. There she goes again, thought Luke, talking as though she had first-hand knowledge of the place.

Maggie left for the market early the next morning, leaving Sarah and Luke in charge of the final party preparations.

"We won't be bored today," Luke said, looking at Maggie's *To Do* list for the party.

"That's good," Sarah said absent-mindedly.

"Do you want to start with getting the food ready or decorating?"

"Sure," Sarah answered as she poured herself another cup of coffee.

"That was a question."

"What? Sorry, I was thinking about something."

Luke knew better than to ask what she was thinking about. "I'll get started on blowing up some of those extra large balloons you thought were such a good idea, if you want to start working on the fruit and veggie trays. I'm not very creative when it comes to arranging vegetables."

Sarah worked all day making sure everything was ready for the party, and Luke could tell that she wanted everything to go well for her grandfather's special day. He also knew she didn't hear half of what he said. More than once he had found her staring into space, not even aware that he was in the same room, not to mention trying to carry on a conversation.

⟡

That evening Sarah drifted among the guests, her smile firmly in place. But her mind was far away. She was desperate to go back to the eighteenth century. The quill box was in her shoulder bag; she just had to wait for the right moment to slip off to the dyke. She had already told her grandparents that she would stay over one more night, so she could help with cleaning up after the guests leave. Luke would drive her home in the morning on his way to the market.

Sarah listened as her grandfather told yet another group

of neighbours the story of his accident. That day seemed like years ago, but it was wonderful to see her grandfather enjoying himself. She was still deep in thought when Maggie announced that there was one final surprise of the evening. That was Sarah's cue. She ran into the kitchen where her painting was hidden in the pantry and brought it out to the verandah. Luke set up the easel in front of her grandfather.

"Is this what I think it is?" Pete White beamed with anticipation.

Sarah carefully set the painting on the easel. For a few moments it was as if no one else existed. She didn't have to ask what he thought. She could see it in his warm chestnut eyes. The joy, the pride and the absolute love of her grandfather wrapped around her like a warm blanket. Sarah breathed a sigh of relief. For that moment, nothing else mattered.

When the last guest had finally departed, Sarah quickly dashed up the stairs. She grabbed her shoulder bag which contained her notes and the special quill box. An electric current tingled through her body. She knew she would never forgive herself if she didn't at least try to reach Anne, but she was scared.

Quietly Sarah climbed the skinny stairs to the attic. She wanted to go over the critical dates one more time. She was thinking of taking her notes with her, but she wasn't sure if they'd survive. She used a flashlight to read through the pages, not wanting anyone to know she was in the attic.

September 5th was the date when the men were tricked into being imprisoned in the church. On October 8th, soldiers started filling the boats with Acadian families, but they didn't actually set sail until October 13th. September 5th, October 8th, and October 13th were the critical dates she needed to remember. She moved to the little window and leaned against the ledge. The stars shimmered like tiny jewels on the velvet night sky. "I'm on my way, Anne."

"Did you say something?"

Sarah jumped at the sound of Luke's voice. "You scared me half to death. How long have you been standing here?"

"Why? What's the big deal?"

"I'm a little jittery tonight, that's all. You startled me." Sarah looked toward Luke's anxious face. His voice was lighthearted, but she could see the concern in his eyes. She wished she could make him understand why Anne's family was so important to her, why she had to try to go back. As she attempted to find words for her thoughts, he pulled her towards him and kissed her. She felt the pressure of his warm lips on hers and then she quickly pulled away. "I have to go, Luke," she blurted. "I'll talk to you when I get back." She heard Luke's voice call to her as she fled down the stairs and out into the cool evening.

Chapter 14

"Sarah!" Luke called from the attic. "Can we talk?" There was no answer.

"What's going on, Luke?" Maggie shouted up the stairs. "Sarah just tore out the door like the house is on fire. Is something wrong?"

"No, I don't think so." At least he hoped there wasn't. Luke pounded down the stairs two at a time. "I just need to talk to her."

"It's kinda late . . ." Luke heard Maggie's voice as the screen door snapped shut behind him. He could see Sarah across the field heading toward the dyke. "What is her bloody obsession with that dyke?" he muttered. Luke cut through the field and onto the dyke where Sarah stood. The moon hung like a silver globe over her head, but she didn't appear to be looking at the moon. Luke stood beside her now, although she did not acknowledge him. That's when he noticed the quill box clutched in her hand. "Sarah, we have to talk."

Sarah closed her eyes and took the lid off the little container. Her knees buckled and she stumbled. Luke grabbed her arm quickly to prevent her from falling. Just then a wind came out of nowhere. The icy gust almost pushed them right off the dyke. He clung tightly to her as the furious wind lashed them with its frigid breath. He had never experienced anything like it. It whipped wildly around them as though they were in a wind tunnel. Everything went black as the roar of the wind consumed them. Then, just as quickly, it was gone. The world gradually came into focus again.

"Man! That was one wild ride." Luke gave his head a shake. "Are you okay?"

"Just surprised." Sarah smiled.

"Yeah, that wind caught me off guard too."

Sarah looked to the horizon where the telltale light of grey dawn was beginning to erase the night. The familiar stand of trees had once again replaced the open field where Maggie's house should have been. She gazed up at the Acadian sky and was surprised to see the ghost of a crescent moon fading from sight.

"How bizarre," Sarah whispered.

"You're not kidding." Luke was looking toward the stand of trees. "Where did those trees come from?" But Sarah was only half listening. She hadn't expected Luke to follow her. Stunned by his kiss, she hadn't wanted him to see how flustered she was. But when she got to the dyke she had heard a voice off in the distance. At first she thought it was Maggie, but as the voice got closer Sarah recognized it unmistakably as Anne's. She had looked around, wondering if Anne had somehow crossed the centuries and vaguely remembered seeing Luke approaching the dyke. After that everything happened quickly. She remembered taking the lid off the quill box and stumbling. That's when Luke grabbed her — just as the wind swept them into its grip.

"Hey! Where did those soldiers come from?" He pointed toward Minas Basin. "It's like we just walked onto a movie set or something."

"Oh no! It's already happening. I have to find Anne!" Sarah started running toward the trees. Glancing back she noticed the confused expression on Luke's face. "Quick, Luke. We have to get into the woods before they see us."

"Sarah!" Luke called. "What's going on? You're starting to freak me out."

"Hurry!" she yelled over her shoulder.

"What's going on?" Luke repeated as he caught up to her.

"I'm not sure. I think it was because you held on to me." Sarah cocked her ear, listening closely for sounds that the soldiers were approaching. Hearing none, she relaxed a bit.

"I have no idea what you're talking about." Luke leaned against a large maple tree and shook his head.

"I know you're not going to like this, and if it's my fault I'm sorry, but we're in the eighteenth century. I wish I knew the date. That's why I have to find Anne." Sarah started to leave.

"Whoa! Not so quickly," Luke said.

The clopping of horses' hooves drew closer, and Sarah motioned for Luke to be quiet. She could see the sharp contrast of the soldier's red coats through the trees.

"Well, it won't be long now, poor beggars," the one closest to them said.

"Poor beggars, indeed!" A gruff voice replied. "Bunch of lazy frogs if you ask me. Lawrence is wise to rid the place of them, I say."

"Come on," Sarah motioned to Luke after the soldiers had passed. "The sun is coming up. We have to get out of here before someone sees us."

Luke looked at his watch. "It's 10 o'clock. The sun has just gone down."

"You tell the sun that. I have other things on my mind."

Luke squinted toward the horizon. "This is insane. How did I get caught up in your crazy dream? When I wake up I'm going to a shrink!"

As they reached the clearing, Luke stopped dead in his tracks. "This is . . ."

"This is the LeBlanc farm," Sarah said matter-of-factly.

"The painting," Luke mumbled, too shocked to get out more than a couple of words.

"We'll hide in the barn for now until I can figure out how to find Anne."

They were barely inside the barn when Sarah spotted Anne leaving the little cottage.

"Thank goodness," Sarah whispered under her breath. "Anne! Anne!" she called in a loud whisper as she hovered just inside the barn door.

Anne looked startled at first but broke into a large grin. "Sarah!" she shrieked. The two girls embraced tightly, oblivious for the moment to Luke's presence. It felt so good to see Anne again. She smelled of fresh bread and marigolds.

"Too bad you missed the betrothal ceremony. Look!" She pulled out a small wooden cross hanging from a fine strip of leather. "François made it for me as a betrothal gift. Feel how smooth it is." She held it out for Sarah to touch, then turned it over. "Do you see? It has my initials 'A H' for Anne Hébert carved inside a heart." She sighed. "I hope the church wedding will be soon." She stopped suddenly as though she had just noticed Luke. "And who is this?" Anne pointed with excitement to Luke who was looking more than a little uncomfortable.

"It's my friend, Luke. Luke, this is Anne, the Acadian friend I told you about."

Luke nodded and reached out to shake Anne's hand.

Anne giggled. "Ooh! He is very tall," she whispered to Sarah, "and very handsome!"

Finally Anne took her eyes off Luke and launched into another rapid-fire speech. "Things have gotten bad here since you left. Soldiers came and took all our weapons and our canoes. The men can't even hunt or fish, and the wild animals are always eating our crops. Now the soldiers have taken over the church. Colonel Winslow moved into Father Landry's house. Have you gone by the church yet? It's not a holy building anymore. Soldiers are camped everywhere. It is the most horrible thing."

"That's terrible." Sarah glanced at Luke to see if he was following any of what Anne was saying. The serious expression on his face suggested he was.

"The men have been called to a meeting this afternoon," Anne continued. "Soldiers have posted notices on the church door and all through the village. Nobody knows what it's about, but it must be serious. There are severe consequences for any who don't attend. I think the men will be asked again to sign that oath of allegiance. It's always about that."

Sarah's heart sank at the mention of the meeting. Today must be September 5th.

"Oh! How stupid of me!" Anne slapped her head with her hand. "Here I am talking away and you have no clothes to wear. I'll go and get your clothes from the chest. Maman will be so happy to see you. You should see her. She takes the clothes out and looks at them and holds them against her cheek, muttering about Jean-Paul's *ange gardienne* and then folds them carefully and puts them back in the chest. It's sad, really, but now you're here!" Anne muttered over and over how tall Luke was. Suddenly her face brightened.

"I know. I will get some things from François. His father is taller and bigger than Papa. He isn't quite as tall as Luc; *alors*, it will do. Maybe I can catch François before he leaves to work on the house. Did I tell you that we're building our own home near Philippe and Monique? So much to tell! But I must hurry." With that final gush of words and a quick hug she flew out the door.

"Whew! Does that girl ever breathe?" Luke asked after Anne had gone.

"Hardly ever." Sarah attempted a smile. Any good feelings of seeing her Acadian friend had quickly evaporated with news of the meeting.

"I thought my French was pretty good," Luke commented. "But she used a lot of words I've never heard before."

"Yeah, the eighteenth-century French is quite different from the French we learned at school, isn't it?"

"Eighteenth-century French?"

Sarah shook her head in disbelief. "You still don't get it, do you? Just where do you think those English soldiers came from? And this barn? And the cute little cottage where Maggie's house should be?"

"I don't have a clue." Luke walked over to the doorway

and peered out. "It doesn't make sense. You can't go back in time. It's impossible. If you could, people would go back all the time."

"I didn't say I understood it," Sarah said, exasperated. "But whether you accept it or not, the fact is, we are now in the eighteenth century."

Luke sat down on a stack of hay and stared blankly at the barn walls as though he didn't hear her.

"Luke," Sarah sat down beside him. "Did you hear what Anne said? The meeting is this afternoon. Do you realize what meeting that is?"

"If today is September 5, 1755, I do. I've read it a million times at the interpretive centre. That's the day all the men and boys over ten were tricked into captivity, which means we'd better take the first time-machine home."

"The *time machine* is my grandfather's little quill box and it's staying with me. I came back to help Anne's family and I'm not leaving until I do."

Luke got up, paced over to the doorway and back. "This is nuts," he muttered under his breath. "I can't believe we're actually in the eighteenth century."

Before long Anne was back. She dumped a large sack of clothes on the clean hay.

Luke took one look at the assortment of clothes, then glared at Sarah. "You don't expect me to actually wear these goofy things do you? I'm out of here." He headed toward the door.

"You can't go out there dressed like that. Someone will see you. And anyway, where will you go?"

"Back to where I came from, that's where."

"It's not that simple, Luke."

"What's the matter?" Anne looked confused. "Doesn't Luke like his clothes? I know they're not that clean but . . ."

"They're just different from what he's used to." Sarah turned toward Luke. "You're going to put us both in a lot of danger if you don't put on these clothes. I'm serious." Sarah felt her patience wearing thin. "We could both be locked up or worse."

Luke muttered under his breath as he grabbed the pile of weird-looking clothes and went into an empty stall while Sarah quickly pulled on her Acadian outfit. Luke managed to get the breeches on, although they barely came to below his knees, and he wasn't too sure about the flap in the front. François' father, Pierre, was a stocky build so the clothes hung loosely.

"I hope this charade is going to be over soon," Luke said, waving the colourful orange sash that was supposed to go around his waist. "I look like an idiot!"

Sarah decided there was no point in trying to convince him otherwise. She thought he looked pretty cool in the open-necked linen shirt that revealed his tanned chest, but she didn't think he was in the mood to hear that just then.

"Does Luke speak any French?" Anne asked. "If Papa thinks he's English it won't be a good thing."

"Yeah, my French is okay," Luke answered in English, "but it doesn't sound like Anne's. Her father will probably figure out I'm not Acadian all by himself."

"We better say he is your brother," Anne added. "Maman and Papa won't like it that you have come with a boy. But if he is your brother . . ."

Sarah nodded. "That's fine."

Luke's only response was to roll his eyes.

"I have to go help my sister-in-law cook for the men who are working on our house. You should come," Anne invited.

Sarah glanced nervously at Luke. "Maybe in a bit. Luke and I have some things to talk over."

Anne gave a knowing smile. "Well, don't be too long. I can't wait to tell everyone that you're here with your brother!"

Sarah watched Anne skip across the field to her brother's house, looking more like a schoolgirl than a betrothed young woman.

Chapter 15

Sarah felt nauseous and it wasn't just the smell of the barn. She had come back with the hopes of somehow helping Anne and her family, but now that she was here the task seemed more daunting than ever.

Luke inspected the crude tools that hung from the walls of the barn as though he were trying to get his head around what had just happened.

"Any ideas about how to approach this whole thing?" Sarah asked hesitantly.

"If that meeting today is the one we think it is, we have to get out of here and soon," Luke answered. "It's not exactly the best time for soaking up the local history."

"Don't you think we should at least warn Anne's family that this meeting is just a trick to get them all into the church?"

Luke looked thoughtful. "Do you think it would make a difference?" For once his tone wasn't sarcastic.

Sarah sighed. "I hope it will." Her voice was barely a whisper. "Let's check out the notice for ourselves," she suggested. "We could use the fresh air."

"You got that right." Luke rose from his prickly seat on the hay.

It took just over twenty minutes to walk to the village church on the dusty road. Luckily, they encountered only a couple of soldiers on horseback who passed them without a second glance. Anne was right about the little church looking more like a military camp than a holy building. Dozens of scarlet coats swarmed the humble building like wasps around a hive. Wooden pickets enclosed the area, with tents pitched for the soldiers' quarters. "It looks like they plan to stay awhile," Sarah said.

Luke nodded. "According to Winslow's diary, it's still quite a while before the transport ships arrive."

"I know. October 8th was the date that they actually started filling the ships with families. I went over all my notes from the archives before I left so that I wouldn't be totally clueless about what was going on." They walked up to the door of the church where the order was posted. It was written in French but there was no question as to the content. It was dated September 2, 1755, and demanded all men and boys over ten attend an important meeting at three o'clock in the afternoon on September 5, 1755. Anyone not in attendance would lose everything.

"Ignorant fools!" sneered one of the soldiers walking by.

"They probably can't even read what it says," added another, chuckling as though it were a great joke.

Sarah bit back the urge to respond. This was definitely not the time to attract extra attention. Still, the comments really burned her.

"That's it," Sarah spoke quietly as they walked away from the church. "Those ignorant soldiers just gave me a brilliant idea. We'll tell Anne's family that we overheard the English soldiers talking. They'd believe that wouldn't they?"

"I thought you didn't want them to know we speak English."

"True," Sarah admitted. "But maybe we'll have to risk it."

Luke didn't look convinced. "The English aren't too popular around here at the moment."

"Anne will stick up for us."

"Then will you agree to go home? I don't particularly want to be herded into the church with all the Acadian men."

"Agreed. I'm not too keen on a long ship voyage myself."

As they neared the LeBlanc farm Jeanne spotted them from the garden. The next moment she was running across the fields at lightning speed, her little brother close behind.

"Sarah!" Jeanne shrieked, as she took a flying leap into Sarah's arms almost knocking her over. Jean-Paul stood back timidly.

"Look at you!" Sarah put Jeanne down and ruffled Jean-Paul's hair. "You're taller already!"

She introduced Luke as her brother to the curious youngsters. Jean-Paul never took his eyes off Luke, but Jeanne raced to the house to spread the news. "Maman! Maman! It's Jean-Paul's angel. She came back!"

Maman appeared in the doorway and waved. "*Le bon Dieu*! It's true, then." When they reached the stoop, Maman smothered Sarah in a hug.

Sarah introduced Luke once more and quickly went on to tell about how they had just arrived from Port Royal. Out of the corner of her eye she saw Luke's look of surprise. Perhaps her eighteenth-century accent was improving.

"You will stay with us then," Maman stated. "Stay for as long as you wish."

"Thank you," Sarah replied, ignoring Luke's raised eyebrows.

"Anne is down at her brother's place. Have you seen her new home?"

"Not yet," Sarah answered, not mentioning that she had already seen Anne.

"Come, we are going there now to feed the hard workers. You must join us."

"We'd love to."

François noticed them coming and set down his tools to shake hands with Luke and Sarah. "A little bird told me you had come to visit."

Pierre Hébert and Charles LeBlanc also stopped working on the shingles to greet the two guests.

"We have come at a bad time, I guess, with all the soldiers and everything," Sarah commented.

"Yes, anytime the English come, it's a bad time," François answered. "What kind of man takes over the home of the priest and turns a holy house into a place of arms?" He shook his head in disgust but then just as quickly his face brightened. "Go to Philippe's and get Anne. She'll want to show you inside. I'll be in big trouble if I go ahead without her."

Anne practically flew from her brother's house when she saw them approaching. "You have to see it, Sarah!" Anne said excitedly. "It has two rooms as well as the loft. François is very clever. The fireplace will be in the middle so that it will heat both rooms." Sarah had never seen anyone this animated about a two-room house.

After they looked at the newly constructed cottage, Sarah and Luke joined the others for the noon meal. The women had prepared a thick soup of carrots, turnips and potatoes which they served with fresh bread and a jug of molasses. Sarah had no appetite for any of it. All she could think about was the news that she would share, news that would not be welcome or possibly even believed.

"You have come from Port Royal, my wife tells me." Papa's eyes rested on Luke.

"Yes," Luke answered.

"What is the news there?"

"There is trouble everywhere right now," Luke answered carefully. "The English soldiers have moved into that area as well."

"We will not talk about the English soldiers," Maman said firmly. "There are little ones at the table and we want to enjoy our meal. You men talk about the soldiers another time."

"My apologies." Pink colour crept into Luke's cheeks.

"Nonsense. It's not your fault."

"Why are the soldiers in our church, Papa?" Jeanne asked.

"Didn't I just say we would not talk of such things?" Maman's voice rose in pitch.

"The English soldiers are in charge of our land," Monsieur LeBlanc continued despite his wife's angry glower. "They have just come to check it over. They have no place to stay, so they are staying at the church. That's all. And now," he smiled sweetly at his wife, "we will have no more talk of soldiers."

Sarah knew her disclosure would also need to wait for a more appropriate time. After the baked apple dessert was served, it appeared that she would get her opportunity. The children left the table and the men quickly began discussing the upcoming meeting at the church. Sarah remained seated at the table when the other women rose to clear away the dishes. Her stomach churned nervously, but she knew it was now or never.

"Luke and I overheard some soldiers talking this morning," she began slowly.

Everyone stared, surprised that Sarah would join the men's conversation. Monsieur LeBlanc looked to Luke for confirmation. "Is this true? What did you hear?"

"It's all a trick." Sarah didn't give Luke a chance to reply. "They intend to keep you all prisoners in the church."

"That's what they said?" Monsieur Hébert shook his head in disbelief.

"It wouldn't surprise me," François replied. "It sounds like something those lying pigs would do."

"Why would they want to lock us up?" Philippe looked worriedly at his wife, Monique. They were expecting their first child soon.

"Probably another attempt to force us to sign their foolish oath." Monsieur LeBlanc's tone was serious.

"Yes," Monsieur Hébert agreed. "That could very well be the plan. They imprisoned the delegates we sent to Halifax to get our weapons back because they wouldn't sign an unconditional oath of allegiance on our behalf. They're still imprisoned on St. George's Island."

"It's worse than that." Sarah's voice cracked with emotion.

Anne joined her friend at the table. "What is it, Sarah? What is going to happen?"

Sarah drew in a deep breath. "The transport ships that are anchored at the mouth of the Gaspereau River are going to take you far from here. Colonel Winslow has orders to remove you all from Grand-Pré." There, she had said it.

"They wouldn't do such a thing, would they Charles?" Madame LeBlanc's face squeezed into a frown. "This is our land, our home." She turned to Sarah, "You must have misunderstood."

"Perhaps my wife has a good point," Charles addressed Sarah this time. "Weren't the soldiers speaking English?"

"Luke and I understand English very well."

"Our father was a merchant," Luke interjected. "He learned English to trade with the ships from Boston, and he thought it was important for us to learn English as well." He paused. "What Sarah says is true. We thought you should know."

In the silence that followed, Sarah was sure everyone could hear her heart pounding, and then they were all talking at once. Finally Charles LeBlanc pushed his chair away from the table and stood. "Pierre and I need to discuss this further. Philippe and François, you are welcome to join us." He rested his hand on Luke's shoulder. "You too, Luke. We will go to Basil, the blacksmith's, and find out what he has heard."

"Let's go," Anne whispered to Sarah after the dishes were done. "Aren't you anxious to know what the men are talking about?"

Sarah nodded. She hoped that someone would believe

her story and convince the others. It took only a few minutes to get to the blacksmith shop. Sarah could hear the men's voices before they reached the doorway. By the sounds of it, several more men had joined the impromptu gathering.

"Charles, you've read the notice. If we don't attend they'll take all our crops, our homes, everything."

"He's right," another said. "They've already taken our muskets and our boats. I believe they are serious."

"And what if these young visitors speak the truth? What if we are all held captive, as they say? Is that not also a possibility?" Sarah recognized Monsieur LeBlanc.

"Well, perhaps it is, but then we will fight. There are more of us than there are of them and our Mi'kmaq friends would not mind taking on those dirty redcoats. They have made that clear to us."

"That was François," Anne whispered.

"With no weapons?" another voice asked. "That would not be so easy."

"Maybe not, but as I see it, we have no choice." Sarah thought that was Monsieur Hébert, but couldn't be sure. "I will not be responsible for putting my family in harm's way," he continued. "It was good of you to give us this information, Charles, but I must go to the meeting."

There were several voices in agreement with this final statement, but then Anne pulled Sarah away from the doorway before she could hear anything else. "It wouldn't do to be caught listening in on the men's meeting. Papa would be most upset about that. He hates it when the women interfere in men's business."

"But surely this is not just men's business," Sarah said as they quickly made their way back toward the LeBlanc cottage. "Everyone in the whole village will be affected."

"I know, but still it is the man's responsibility to protect his family."

As they neared the cottage they could see Maman on the doorstep frantically waving her hands for them to hurry. "Where have you been? It's bad enough that Papa is busy with talking and more talking all day long. Do you want to starve all winter? There is much work to be done. We need to gather the vegetables out of the garden. It's time to put them in the root cellar. I also don't want the soldiers to help themselves to our food."

Sarah's heart was a lead weight as she dug turnips out of the cold ground. In all her researching and planning to return to Anne's time it had never really dawned on her that she might arrive while the deportation was taking place. How could she expect the men instantly to come up with an escape plan when the meeting was in a couple of hours? No, she had come too late. The LeBlancs would not believe the horrible fate that awaited them until it was already upon them. Luke's words echoed in her mind. *You can't change history.*

Chapter 16

The church bell tolled ominously throughout the valley announcing the three o'clock meeting. Sarah and Anne came out to the front stoop to watch the procession of men, young and old, as they drifted through the fields and across the dyke to the church. Soon Luke joined them.

"I talked to your father again, Anne, but I don't think he believes that the English would do such a thing. He keeps mentioning all the other times that they were called to meetings to discuss the signing of the oath."

"There just isn't enough time for him to think about it," Sarah commented. "The bell is already calling them. We're too late."

"Don't talk like that," Anne implored. "You make it sound like someone is dying."

Sarah squeezed her friend's hand. "I'm sorry. Sometimes I should keep my thoughts to myself." She looked to the sky where heavy cloud blocked the sun making it darker than usual for mid-afternoon. How fitting.

The door to the cottage swung open. "We're off to our meeting." Monsieur LeBlanc tried to sound casual, as though it were a common occurrence.

"Don't go yet," Anne pleaded. "Wait to find out what the soldiers have planned."

"I have to go, my little sparrow, otherwise I'll put the whole family at risk."

Anne buried her head in her father's chest. "I still wish you wouldn't go."

Madame LeBlanc dabbed her eyes with her apron. "At least leave Mathieu here. He is just a boy."

"Maybe so, but he is a boy well past ten years. You know what the order says. Do you want all our land to be confiscated or worse?"

Madame LeBlanc shook her head. "I still don't understand why they need the young boys. It's not right."

Monsieur LeBlanc's voice softened. "No harm will come to him, I promise." His gaze then fell on Luke. "If the meeting goes longer than we expect will you watch over my family?"

Sarah could tell that the question had caught Luke totally off guard.

"I'll do my best," he replied.

Just how was he planning to do that from the twenty-first century? Sarah wondered. Still, she didn't know how else he could have answered the question.

Monsieur LeBlanc kissed his wife, then he and Mathieu joined the others who were making their way to the church. Mathieu turned and waved to his mother. He looked pleased to be invited to such an important meeting. Sarah felt sorry for him. He had no idea what was in store for him in the coming days and weeks.

Madame LeBlanc watched with the others until her husband and son were out of sight, then she turned to go inside. "Don't be long, Anne. The men aren't the only ones with important things to do. Nobody wants to come home to a supper still wearing its feathers, eh?" Madame LeBlanc chuckled at her joke though her face looked weary.

After her mother went inside, Anne stared off in the direction of the orchard. "François said he would let me know what he had decided, either way."

"Do you think he will defy the order?" Sarah asked.

"I don't know. It's very difficult to go against your parents. And what if something awful did happen to his family because of it? I don't think he could live with that."

Moments later François strode up the well-worn path to the house. "Are you going to the church, Luc?"

"No. My name won't be on any of the lists."

"Do you think they'll check the lists before they shoot when they see a man roaming free?"

"That's a good point, Luke," Sarah commented. "You better stay out of sight once this meeting gets started."

"You are welcome to use our cottage if you wish," François offered. "Perhaps you would like a space away from all these women?"

"I would very much appreciate having a roof over my head," Luke answered. "And the LeBlanc cottage is a little crowded." Both young men laughed.

"And you, François?" Anne asked. "What have you decided?"

"I'll walk into the trap with the others," he said matter-of-factly. "Papa has given me little choice. If I run, they will think I'm selfish and a coward."

Anne looked away, unable to look him in the eye. François lifted Anne's chin gently, forcing their eyes to meet. "It doesn't mean that the English have won. We won't give up."

After François left for the church, Anne found some linens and blankets for Luke to take to the cottage.

"I'll bring you some supper this evening," Sarah promised. "We'll talk about our plans then. It's going to be a long night for everyone, I think."

"Yes." Luke nodded solemnly. "It is going to be one of many long nights, unfortunately."

Supper was a dismal event. Anne's mother had put off the meal as long as possible, waiting for the return of her men, but eventually she realized that they would have to go ahead and eat. Evening prayers were equally sombre without Papa LeBlanc in his usual role.

"Madame LeBlanc, do you mind if I take Luke some supper now?" Sarah asked.

"*Madame LeBlanc* — so formal. Please call me Maman. By all means, we will pack a supper for Luke right now." She started to get up from the spinning wheel where she was preparing to spin the combed flax into thread. "With all my worrying I forgot about him."

"I can get it ready. You carry on with your work."

"Why have they not returned?" Maman asked above the whirring of the spinning wheel. "What more can there possibly be to talk about?"

"They're not coming back," Anne answered wearily. She set down her knitting. "Sarah and Luke tried to warn Papa but he wouldn't listen."

The spinning wheel slowed to a stop. "Your Papa and I, we are not so young anymore. Everything we own, everything we have worked for is here. This year we have the best harvest we have ever had. We can't risk everything."

There was a soft knock at the door and in walked Anne's oldest brother, Philippe. He slumped down at the table looking tired and defeated, but Maman didn't appear to notice his sadness.

"You're back!" She kissed the top of his head. "Where are Papa and Mathieu? The stew is keeping warm over the fire. I'll get you some."

"Sorry, Maman." Philippe shook his head in despair.

"But, what is going on? I don't understand?" Maman threw her hands up in the air.

"Sarah and Luke were right. The meeting was a trick to get all the men into the church. They aren't going to let us go. I have only a few moments. A few of us were given permission to let the families know what is going on and to request food for the men."

Maman's shoulders shook and she covered her face with her hands. "This cannot be."

Philippe continued, "They know that the women and children won't go anywhere as long as the men are captive in the church. Even so, the whole village is being patrolled, just to make sure no one is trying to escape."

"Such nonsense. I don't know why we would escape. This is our home. Just sign their foolish oath or whatever they want so they will let you go."

"It's not that simple now." Philippe rose from the table and wrapped his arms around his mother. "Be strong, Maman. We'll get through this. I have to go now. There are some more families I need to inform."

"What about the food? How will you get it?"

"Bring it to the church. The soldiers have promised that they will let you bring it to us."

Maman dabbed her eyes with the corner of her apron. "We won't let you go hungry. I'm going to bring the stew to the church right now."

Philippe kissed his mother on the cheek and disappeared out the door.

Maman sat crumpled on the chair like a worn-out rag, the lines in her face etched into ever deepening crevices.

Sarah thought of her own mother's smooth, almost flawless skin, thanks to countless jars of anti-aging creams and weekly facials. The two women were probably close to the same age.

When Sarah took Luke's supper to him she told him about Philippe's visit. He shook his head grimly. "This is only the beginning. There is still a long road ahead."

"It's all so discouraging." Sarah sat by the cold fireplace on a blanket she had brought with her. "I didn't plan to arrive right when everyone was being imprisoned. Now it seems rather pointless."

"When did you plan to arrive, if you don't mind my asking?"

Sarah smiled in spite of herself. "I know it sounds ridiculous, but I didn't consider the possibility of arriving in the middle of the deportation. I guess I don't really understand how the timing works. I mean, when I got back to Maggie's after my last experience, no time had transpired. It's odd."

"Well, I can't help you there. Time Travel 101 was completely booked last term, so I didn't take it."

Sarah groaned. "I don't know how you can even think of jokes at a time like this."

Luke's face turned serious. "I didn't plan to time travel anywhere, but that's a little irrelevant now. The point is, we are here, so what are we going to do?"

"You mean we're not going to leave tonight?"

"First of all, we would be crazy to go anywhere tonight.

Winslow and his men will be particularly diligent right now, I would think. Secondly, you heard what I said to Charles LeBlanc. I promised I would watch over his family."

"But the 'meeting' isn't going to be over until the ships sail." Sarah didn't want to admit that she hadn't really thought he was serious when he made that promise. "I agree with you, though. We should at least stay for a few days until Maman LeBlanc has a better idea about what is going on. Perhaps I can get the women together and help them prepare food and herbs for the long ship voyage and you can help with the daily chores so that we have more time to gather necessary supplies." Sarah perked up. Maybe, she thought, her returning to this century would not be in vain after all.

Chapter 17

The next morning Maman already had some loaves ready for the oven by the time Sarah came down from the loft. Sometimes Sarah wondered if the woman ever slept. No matter how early she got up, Maman had already tended the fire and had some other task well under way.

Sarah took a deep breath before broaching the subject of a women's meeting. She wasn't sure she would get a positive response. Well, there's no time like now-time, Sarah thought. It was one of her mother's favourite sayings and Sarah was surprised that it popped into her head just then. She had to admit she'd barely had time to think about her mother these days.

"Maman LeBlanc, I would like to talk to you about something very important," Sarah ventured cautiously.

"Ah, and does this have to do with the English soldiers?" Maman wiped her hands on her apron and sat down at the table.

Sarah plunged right in, not waiting for further invitation. "More ships will arrive at Minas Basin, and when they do you will join the men on the ships and be sent far from here."

Maman gave her a curious look. "I don't know how you foresee such things, but you have been right about many things." Maman raised her hands in the air. "God works in mysterious ways, does he not? Perhaps you have been sent to tell us these things."

Sarah continued, "The journey will be a long one, and there are certain foods and medicines that everyone should bring to prevent sickness. Do you think we could invite some of the other women to a meeting here so that we can talk about what is important to bring?"

Maman laughed at this suggestion. "Women meeting to talk about things? Whoever heard of such a thing! It's always the men who have important meetings."

"We don't have to call it a meeting. The women like to visit each other."

"Yes, yes, of course." Maman fell silent for a moment. "With all my heart, precious one, I hope that you are wrong. But what harm could it do for us to prepare some things?"

The meeting time was set for the next afternoon. That

would give the women the morning for chores. Everyone was feeling the panic of winter approaching with their men folk being unable to help.

Maman was worried too, and Sarah knew she appreciated having her and Luke to help with the work. Even so, it was difficult for her to adjust to having a man in her kitchen.

"Leave those chickens for me," she insisted one afternoon when she caught Luke plucking them in preparation for chicken pie. "There are three women here, and we can't manage to prepare the meals? I've never heard of anything so ridiculous."

Luke didn't quit. "I think I'm doing a fair job with these chickens," he said. "I won't try to make the pies, though."

Maman clicked her tongue in disapproval, but she let him finish the chickens. It was the same with all the household jobs with which Luke helped. Maman complained a lot, but secretly Sarah knew she was glad of the help.

The morning before the meeting, Luke announced that he was going down to the cottage to pick some berries in the bushes close by. "I'll camouflage my clothes and stay close to the edge of the forest so that I won't be easily seen," he told Sarah. "I need to get out for a bit, and a women's meeting would be the perfect time to make myself scarce."

"Why don't you disguise yourself as a woman?" Sarah suggested.

"With stubble like this?" Luke rubbed his chin with his fingers. "I don't think I'd fool anyone."

"I wouldn't get too close to the soldiers if I were you, but from a distance no one would suspect anything."

"I'm sure Maman has an extra dress and kerchief you could borrow," Anne added.

"Just because I agreed to do women's work, doesn't mean I want to look like a woman," Luke protested.

Maman chuckled. "Come, it won't be so bad. This is no time for pride. It is more important that you are safe." With that she went over to a chest and pulled out a print dress for Luke to put on. As he reluctantly pulled the dress over his breeches Sarah couldn't help thinking what a shame it was that the camera would not be invented until the next century.

After Luke left, Sarah and Anne went about the steamy job of making soap. The supply of soap had almost run out and soap would definitely be needed aboard the crowded ships. Anne got the pail of cracklings from the root cellar and dumped them into the big cauldron on the fire. She then sprinkled the lye crystals on the fat and added the water. Sarah stirred the fat mixture while Anne fished out the bits of meat that were mixed in with the fat. Every few minutes Anne checked to see if the consistency was right. Sarah brushed the damp hair off her forehead and thought about the meeting that afternoon. She hoped the women would understand the importance of what she was going to talk to them about, and she hoped they'd believe her.

Finally Anne declared the soap mixture the right consistency, and they poured it into flat tubs to be cooled and cut into bars later.

Sarah felt nervous that afternoon as they arranged chairs and prepared for the meeting, but she needn't have worried. Within minutes of their stepping inside the door, Maman told everyone the purpose of the meeting. All the women were happy for a chance to get together and share bits of news they had heard.

Sarah watched the faces of the women when she told her story. She could tell that many of the women did not believe her, but they listened politely. They weren't prepared to give up hope — not yet. Still, they did suggest some priorities for foods and medicines to have on hand. Sarah stressed the need for dried berries, particularly strawberries and blueberries, to prevent illness. That was easily accomplished. Most families had a supply of dried strawberries from the spring harvest, and the blueberry bushes were still heavy with berries, so collecting blueberries in time shouldn't be a problem. Sarah was impressed with Maman's knowledge of herbs. She told the women exactly which plants they needed for treating coughs, upset stomachs and numerous other ailments.

Sarah glanced anxiously out the door of the cottage. They had just finished evening prayers, and there was still no sign of Luke. What if soldiers *had* spotted a suspicious-looking Acadian woman, after all?

"He'll come soon," Anne commented. "It's so quiet in the new cottage, he probably fell asleep and lost track of time."

"I hope you're right."

"Come, I want to show you something," Anne motioned for Sarah to follow her.

They climbed the steep steps to the loft, and then Anne pulled a wooden chest out from the corner. She opened it revealing a beautiful collection of linens and woolens.

"Did you make all of this?" Sarah picked up a bed sheet.

"Maman helped a lot," Anne admitted. "We worked many winters so that I would have things for my own home when the time came. A shadow crossed Anne's face. Who knows when that will be now?"

"One day you'll have your own place, Anne," Sarah said gently, "even if it isn't here." She held up a bright yellow cloth to change the subject. "I love this colour."

Anne smiled. "I told Maman that I didn't want to have plain coverings for my table. Even in winter my home will be bright and cheery."

"Just like you." Sarah smiled warmly at her friend.

"It takes a lot of work to prepare the flax for spinning and weaving into linen but it's worth it. Look at all the beautiful things I have."

"Amazing!" Sarah remembered reading about the process at the Grand-Pré National Historic Site. They had used goldenrod from the fields for the yellow dye.

"Anne, you need to get Jeanne settled into bed now," Maman called upstairs. "Perhaps you could tell Jean-Paul and Jeanne a nice bedtime story. They need to have some happy thoughts for tonight."

"Yes, Maman." Anne lifted one more item out of the chest. "This is the shirt I made for François," she whispered. "It's his wedding shirt."

Sarah was just about to comment on the delicate stitching when she heard voices outside. She peeked out the casement window in time to see two soldiers approach the house.

There was a loud banging on the door, and then soldiers wearing the flashy red coats of the British army pushed their way in uninvited. The girls crouched by the attic hatch to see what was going on.

"Get out of my house, now!" Maman grabbed the poker from the fireplace as a weapon. "You lying kidnappers are not welcome here."

The larger soldier, who was the older of the two, grabbed a loaf of bread from the table and bit off a chunk. The other one, who looked to be no more than Luke's age, glanced around nervously as though he didn't know what he was doing here.

"Orders from Colonel Winslow," the older one barked,

his mouth full of bread. "We are checking for any firearms or tools that could be used as weapons."

Maman didn't understand the soldiers, but she certainly made it clear that whatever they wanted they were not welcome in her home. She waved her hands at them as though shooing an animal out of the room.

"Get out! Get out!"

The loud obnoxious soldier seized the poker from Maman's hand and pushed her roughly, causing her to fall against the table. Maman shrieked and clutched her rosary about her neck.

"*Cochon!*" Anne yelled from the loft.

"Ah, what have we here?"

The girls moved back as far as possible as the doughy, pockmarked face of the soldier appeared through the loft doorway.

"Hey, Thompson! There's one for each of us up here!"

Maman screamed again which momentarily distracted the soldier. Anne grabbed a clay chamber pot from beside the bed. The burly soldier ducked out of the way just in time as it crashed to the floor and smashed into little pieces. Too bad it wasn't full, Sarah thought. She could hear Jeanne's muffled sobs from under the wood-frame bed where she was hiding. Fortunately the soldier was too preoccupied to notice.

"Thompson!" The brute snarled at his young partner. "Don't just stand there like the idiot you are. Hold your musket on the fat wench. And keep that bloody poker away from her or she'll poke yer watery eyes out! Now let's see how brave the sassy wenches are!" He kept his gun trained on the girls as he sauntered casually to Mathieu's side of the room and tore the curtain divider down.

"Let's go, Sir," a shaky voice called from down below. "They don't have any weapons here. You heard the Colonel's orders. No harming the people."

His partner snorted and expelled a low chuckle at this comment. "I'm not going to hurt anyone. I just want some fun, that's all. Even stuffy ol' Winslow wouldn't deprive his men of a little sport, would he?" He laughed a deep throaty laugh.

Sarah shuddered to think what this beast considered fun, but she had no intention of finding out. She threw herself to the floor, ducking the hefty soldier just as he lunged for her. She grabbed one of Anne's wooden shoes from beside the bed and hurled it at him. The shoe found its mark but seemed to bounce off with little effect. He turned quickly and grabbed Anne who was scurrying to the doorway. She yelled and kicked her captor and even managed to bite his scaly hand, causing him to issue a string of colourful obscenities.

"I think this rabid rodent needs to be taught a lesson." He twisted Anne's arm and she let out a sharp gasp. Sarah could see the tears swelling in her friend's eyes.

They would have as much luck fighting this thug as they

would fending off a charging bull. They needed the element of surprise — something to catch him off guard.

"Leave us alone!" Sarah yelled in English, the words exploding from her mouth as she whipped the other shoe into his face. He caught her wrist, but with Anne still kicking and flailing, Sarah was able to wrench herself free.

Glaring suspiciously at Sarah, the soldier tossed the screaming, kicking Anne over his shoulder and clambered down the narrow steps.

Sarah followed quickly behind them. "You heard your partner." Her voice sounded steadier than she felt. "Winslow does not condone harassing the people."

The young soldier looked away from his charge for a moment giving Sarah the opportunity to snatch the poker that lay on the floor.

"Hey, leave that be!" He tried to get it from her, but she was too quick for him.

Maman gave him a hard push then quickly grabbed a knife from one of the drawers. She had fire in her eyes, and Sarah knew Maman intended to use the knife if she needed to. Thompson pointed his musket shakily at Maman and instructed her to drop the knife. But Maman continued to yell and wave the knife in the air. The older soldier tried to take the knife with his right hand while balancing Anne on his shoulder with his left. Sarah gave a hard jab to the back of his legs with the poker. Instinctively he grabbed his leg, dropping Anne to the floor in the process. She scrambled quickly to her feet and away from him.

"You useless excuse for a soldier, do something!" he fumed at Thompson who looked as if he would rather be hanging out with his buddies than dressed in uniform and carrying a firearm.

"You will both be reported for this," Sarah glared at the one called Thompson. "I don't know why you're listening to someone so intent on bringing dishonour to His Majesty's men."

"Ye speak the King's English well for a Frenchy, or are ye a mixed blood?" the ugly one sneered. "Yer more brave than bright I dare say, seein' as we have the weapons and there are no men folk to protect you, hey lassie?"

"Let's go, Manning." The young soldier sounded more hopeful than confident. "They aren't causing any trouble."

"I'd say these qualify as weapons." Manning kicked the end of the poker that Sarah held and gestured toward the knife that Maman had a death grip on. "I'll be taking these and reporting you to the Colonel for disobeying orders."

Sarah stood tall and looked the menacing soldier right in the eye. "I happen to know that Colonel Winslow would be extremely displeased with your actions tonight." She willed her voice to stay calm. "I wouldn't be surprised if the colonel relieved both of you of your duties."

Manning squinted hard at Sarah. "There's something not right about you."

Sarah took a slow, deep breath before continuing. "You'd

be surprised how much I know about this whole opera-tion," she announced boldly, even though her insides had turned to jelly. "You use those weapons and Colonel Wins-low will not deal kindly with you."

"I don't know who you are or what yer doing dressed as a Frenchy, but I mean to find out." He slapped the young soldier called Thompson, on the back. "We were just leav-ing anyway, eh Thompson?" He paused only long enough to spit on the floor on the way out.

Sarah collapsed at the table, her legs shaking violently now. She hoped they had seen the end of the soldiers.

Chapter 18

Sarah pushed a loose strand of hair under her kerchief. The men had only been imprisoned for five days, but it seemed much longer. She was exhausted — they all were. Today the girls took advantage of the bright sun to dry the most recent collection of berries and herbs. Anne covered the tray with a thin mesh to keep the birds and bugs away.

"Do you hear that?" Sarah cocked her ear toward the sound. "It's coming from the direction of the church."

"Yes, it sounds like voices. Do you think the men are coming home?" Anne asked hopefully.

"No, I don't think so." Sarah remembered that Winslow separated the young men from their fathers to try to prevent a revolt.

"Let's go see for ourselves." Anne dipped her hands in the wash bucket and splashed some water on her face.

"I'll meet you out front in a minute," Sarah said. She ran to the fire pit behind the barn where Luke was smoking meat. She wanted to let him know where she and Anne were going. He had been very upset when he had found out about the incident with the soldiers, and had stuck close by ever since.

"Are you sure you should be hanging around there?" Luke asked, when he found out where Sarah and Anne were going.

"We'll stay out of the fray — don't worry. We'll let you know what's up as soon as we get back." Sarah started toward the house and then turned back to Luke. "You're pretty convincing as an Acadian girl. Still, it might be a good time for you to stay out of sight."

"Yeah, I'm just about finished here anyway."

The commotion grew louder as Sarah and Anne neared the main road. Soon the procession of men came into view. Flanked by stone-faced soldiers armed with muskets and bayonets, many of the men looked angry. Others were singing. Some of the men cried out names of loved ones as they caught a glimpse of their families in the crowd that had gathered. Hundreds of women and children lined the dirt road wailing and sobbing. One woman clung to the arm of her husband and refused to let go, but a soldier pushed her roughly aside.

"What's happening? Are they sending the men away

already, without their families?" The colour drained from Anne's face.

"No, I think they are separating the men so that they don't cause trouble," Sarah answered. "They are probably going to put them on one of the ships."

Anne and Sarah spotted François near the end of the line. His head held proudly, he marched with determination, as though he were the captor not the prisoner. Anne's brothers, Mathieu and Philippe, were not far behind. As Sarah had suspected, there was no sign of Anne's or François' father.

"I hope they are planning a revolt," Anne spat the words out. "I hate the English."

The girls walked the rest of the way home in silence. Sarah felt helpless. No words of comfort would solve anything. If only there was more she could do.

*

Maman moved slowly as she brought the hot soup to the table for the evening meal. The children chattered away, innocent of the black mood that hung over the table until Jean-Paul asked when Papa was coming home and Maman burst into tears.

"Don't ask so many questions," Anne chided. Then Jean-Paul exploded into tears and Jeanne ran from the table shouting, "I want Papa to come home." No one ate much after that.

"We'd be foolish to stay much longer," Luke spoke quietly while pouring the steaming water into the wash tub for the dishes.

Sarah nodded. She knew Luke was right. "It's just so hard. They have so much to deal with and . . ."

Luke gently touched her shoulder. "I know. The whole thing is horrible and repulsive. But we can't change anything — not really."

"That's the worst part."

"Let's meet in the barn after dark to make our plans," Luke suggested.

"You aren't thinking we'll go tonight, are you?"

"Maybe you should mention something to Anne, just in case we do decide to leave. It's possible."

Sarah understood Luke was worried. Still, she knew Winslow wouldn't start the first loading of the ships until October 8th, which was still a few weeks away. It wasn't as though they would be caught by surprise.

After the dishes were done, Sarah offered to help deliver food to the men on the ships. "If Anne and I deliver food to the ships, you'll be free to visit Papa and Mathieu at the church," Sarah suggested. Thank goodness the soldiers had had the sense to leave Mathieu with his father, at least.

"What would we do without our guardian angel?" Maman smiled softly. "That is a good idea."

It was strange rowing out to the floating prison, and Sarah felt a little nervous. Once they got there, François and

Philippe were called up on deck to receive their food, but Sarah was surprised at how little supervision there was. François and Philippe chatted freely with them while they ate their meal, and they didn't see another redcoat until they were climbing back into the longboat to head for shore. It was then that a seed of an idea began to grow. It was a wild idea — crazy, risky and downright dangerous — yet Sarah dared to believe that it just might work. She didn't want to say anything to Anne yet, but she was bursting to share her idea with Luke.

As soon as the long boat ground onto the shore, Sarah told Anne that she was meeting Luke later on that evening. "If Maman notices I'm gone, tell her that Luke and I have something very important to talk about. Tell her we have to make plans for travelling soon."

Anne frowned. "I keep forgetting you aren't going with us. I'm going to miss you a lot."

Sarah forced the tears back. "You've been like a sister to me. I'll be lost without you."

Sarah knew it wasn't going to be easy to leave, no matter when they went, but she was all the more determined to make her plan work. She *had* to do something.

⚘

"Let me get this straight." Luke scratched his head as he paced back and forth in the chilly barn. "You're going to have François dress as a woman and walk off the ship while the soldiers watch?"

"I know it sounds crazy," Sarah said, squirming on the loose straw, "but I really think it could work. Picture this. It's already the beginning of October. Two supply ships and one transport have arrived but there are still not enough ships for all the people. Winslow gets impatient. He orders the soldiers to bring the women and children to the shore so that he can start filling the ships he already has. He wants to keep the families together, so he's trying to sort out which of the young men belong to which families."

Luke's eyes narrowed, "Did you read about this by any chance?"

"As a matter of fact I did. When the women know that they are actually being forced out of their homes and are ordered to the shore it will be incredibly chaotic. Women will be going to the shore, then to the ships and back again. François can join one of the groups. By the time Winslow discovers that some men are missing, he won't want to free up soldiers to go hunting through the forests for stray Acadians."

"I give you a lot of credit, Sarah. You've really thought this through," Luke commented. "There's only one small problem."

"Which is?" Sarah prompted.

"You read Winslow's diary, right?"

"Yes, that's where I got a lot of the information. Why?"

"Do you remember reading about an escape attempt by several of the men on the ships? He wrote that they all came back — all but two — and those two didn't exactly escape either. They were shot. What's the point in helping with an escape plan if they're all going to come back anyway?"

"Maybe they didn't all come back," Sarah said. "Maybe Winslow only wrote that to save face. Maybe some of them *did* escape, and Winslow couldn't be bothered to send his men into the forest to find them. Or maybe the two men who did not return were not shot. Maybe Winslow made that up so that he could say no one escaped. Who would know, after all? Winslow is likely the only one keeping a journal of all the events." Sarah felt a surge of confidence course through her veins.

"François did say that the Mi'kmaq would come to their aid if they decided to fight the English," Luke commented. "François and Anne could probably hide out at their camp until it was safe to travel."

"Then we'll try?" Sarah asked. "You'll help Anne and François escape?"

Luke nodded his head. "Let's do it!"

Chapter 19

"Do you really think it will work?" Anne asked after hearing Sarah's escape idea. The girls huddled in the corner of the room so as not to wake Jeanne.

"Yes, I think it will. You've seen how the soldiers let the women come and go as they like. No one even notices how many women are on board at any given time."

"That's true. Oh! I can hardly wait to see what François thinks about your plan. I know he is very angry about what is happening, and he will do anything to avoid being forced to leave L'Acadie on the ship."

The girls whispered late into the night about what they would need to do, and what Anne and François would need if the plan went ahead.

Early the next morning, the girls went to the ship with their baskets of food. They were sent down below to the crowded quarters that housed fifty of the men. Fifty men who had not seen soap or water recently, according to Sarah's nose.

Anne's brother, Philippe, spotted them and cleared a spot for them to place the basket. François was standing in the corner with a group of young men but came over quickly when he saw them. Anne spoke quietly as she dug into the basket for some food. "We have something important to tell you, and we don't want to attract attention. Don't let your face show what you're thinking."

"What is it? What's going on? Is Papa all right?" Philippe's voice was anxious but he kept a composed appearance.

"It's nothing like that," Anne whispered. "We have an idea for you to escape."

"You do?" François looked surprised.

"Yes, it was Sarah's idea."

"I will gladly hear about it. Some of us have been talking about what we can do. This aggression by the English must not be tolerated."

Sarah proceeded to explain the details. Philippe's face was hard to read, but François' enthusiasm beamed through regardless of Anne's warning.

"Yes," he agreed. "Dressing like women is a brilliant idea. Women are always coming and going with food. I think many of the men will be interested in this idea."

Sarah continued, "Colonel Winslow is still waiting for the provision ships. When they arrive, he'll have room to start sorting out the families and filling the ships. There will be a lot of confusion around that time. I'm thinking that will be the best time to escape."

"How do you know all this?" Philippe asked warily.

"She knows," Anne interjected. "You have to trust her. She knew that the meeting was a trick, didn't she?"

François appeared less concerned than Philippe about where Sarah had obtained her information. "I will discuss it with the others tonight, after the soldiers have done their final round." This time he didn't try to conceal his smile.

"You better go now," Philippe told his sister. "You don't want to arouse suspicions."

The girls didn't talk on their way back to shore, but as the water slapped the sides of the longboat, Sarah felt the seed of hope growing in her heart.

-ℓℓ

The days passed in a blur of endless chores. Every day Sarah and Anne made their trip to the ships to bring the food and to talk to François. He and a few of the other men on the ship were helping to plan the details of the escape. Among the Mi'kmaq, Anne's friend Marie proved to be the more helpful with the preparations. Luke and Marie's brothers, Joe and Patrice, worked alongside her at the camp. Anne and Sarah did their best to keep both groups informed. In addition, they had their own huge list of chores. They wanted to be sure Maman had enough supplies, but they also tried to spend a couple of hours a day at the Mi'kmaq camp helping with the work there.

Today, Sarah and Luke were helping Anne make snowshoes, which would be critical with winter approaching. Marie's brother, Joe, had showed Luke how to bend the wood for the frames and Marie demonstrated how to weave the rawhide across the frame for the webbing and how to attach the leather ties for the feet.

After Luke had finished with the frames, he continued his work on the hideouts he and Joe had prepared for the men to use. The Mi'kmaq had been very generous in their contributions of basic supplies so that the men would have a good start.

As Sarah and Anne worked on the snowshoes, Marie described the route to their winter home. Sarah was reminded how strenuous and dangerous this would be. Escaping the ships was one thing. Surviving the journey through the forest with winter fast approaching was entirely another.

When it was time to leave for the day, Luke told Sarah that he had decided to stay the night at the Mi'kmaq camp. There was more work to be done on the shelters, and they were running out of time. Marie's brother, Patrice, walked the girls back to the cottage. Soldiers would be less likely to bother them with the tall Mi'kmaq warrior by their side.

Sarah was already getting out dishes for their evening meal when Madeleine Hébert burst through the door.

"Have you heard the news, Marguerite?"

Startled, Anne's mother practically threw the soup ladle clear across the room. "What news? What have you heard?" She retrieved the spoon from the floor.

"The English soldiers are going to send us away from here on those ships. Can you believe it? Father Landry is telling families all through Grand-Pré that we have to pack up our things and be ready to go on the ships. I never thought they'd go through with such a thing. I thought it was all big talk to get us to sign that oath. What will we do?"

Maman shook her head sadly. "When do we have to be ready?"

"In two days! We have only two days and then they are sending us away on the ships!" Madeleine burst into tears.

"We will survive," Maman assured her. "We will stick together and we will survive." She put her arm around her friend's shoulder. "Gather all your belongings together, and bring the children here. We will stay together, and we will get through this."

"You are a good friend, Marguerite. You are a good friend." Madeleine rose from the table. "I can't leave the children any longer, but I wanted to tell you."

"Don't forget to pack your herbs for medicines and all the dried food we prepared. We have to stay strong."

Sarah was proud of Maman. She was far calmer than Sarah imagined she would be.

ℓℓ

Sarah woke up to the steady drumming of rain on the roof of the cottage. She had fallen into a sound sleep, the first one in weeks, and it took her a moment to remember what day it was.

"Do you hear that rain?" Anne asked Sarah. "What do you think will happen with the escape plans?"

Escape. She sat bolt upright. The word hit her like an electric shock. Today was when the women were supposed to gather on the beach, and today was when the men were going to go through with their plan.

"I'm not sure." Sarah hadn't expected the rain. Had she somehow missed that in her reading? She hurried to get dressed. The room had become very chilly overnight and this morning there was no sun to warm it up.

"They won't make the women and children go to the beach in this downpour, will they?" Anne asked.

"I'm not sure what they'll do. I'm glad we took the clothes to François yesterday. At least we don't need to worry about that."

Anne began packing her belongings in a heavy canvas sack. "I'm going to take this to Marie's wigwam first thing this morning." Anne paused. "I think if my things are already at the camp it will give me extra courage to go through with this. I have never done anything so hard in my whole life." She choked back tears. "Maman is trying to be brave for me; inside she knows this is best for François and me. But I will miss them all dreadfully every day of my life."

Sarah could think of no words to comfort her friend. "Do you want me to come with you?"

"No, you stay here with Maman and help her pack the cart. If they don't get called to the shore today, at least it will be ready."

"When you come back we'll take the food to the ship one more time and check on the men."

"If everything goes as planned, François will leave with me and that will be it. We will go directly to the Mi'kmaq camp."

"I know."

Moments later, Sarah watched her friend lug the heavy sack through the rain toward the forest. Something didn't feel right. She rubbed her arms, trying to rub away the shivers. Perhaps the heavy rain was making everything seem worse, although she doubted that was possible.

Anne had been gone for about half an hour when Madame Hébert arrived at the door with her troop of sopping children. "Come in out of the rain," Maman called, herding the children, muddy clogs and all, into the small room.

"I brought as many things as I could squeeze into this

rickety cart," Madame Hébert said. "It's covered well with heavy skins, but I'll put it in the barn so it will stay dry."

Sarah helped towel off the children and put their wet clothing by the fire to dry, then she continued to organize things for packing in the cart when the weather let up — if it did, she thought.

When Madame Hébert came in from the barn, Maman LeBlanc had hot tea ready for her. "This will calm our ragged nerves," she said as she placed the pot of tea and cups on the table.

"I have more news from Father Landry," Madame Hébert said as she sipped the hot tea. "I told him I was coming straight here so that he could skip your farm. The poor man is completely exhausted with being ordered here and there constantly by that Winslow. Father Landry is the only one who speaks English so he has become their messenger boy."

"Enough about Father Landry." Maman LeBlanc was growing impatient. "What is your news?"

"The rainstorm does not look like it will let up, so they have postponed when we must gather at the beach. We are to go there tomorrow instead."

"Today, tomorrow, it makes little difference now. We'll need to get the meals to the men, though, rain or no rain." No sooner had Maman LeBlanc finished speaking when there was a great thump at the door and a soggy, rough-looking Acadian woman stumbled in.

"*Le bon Dieu!*" Madeleine Hébert exclaimed. "Is that you François? Have they freed you?"

François shook his head and gasped for air. He had apparently run non-stop all the way. "Dressed like this? No, I have not been freed." His eyes swept the room as he pulled off the sopping dress. "Where's Anne? We have to leave immediately. Soon the soldiers will notice that some of us are missing and start searching."

"Anne has taken her things to the Mi'kmaq camp. She'll be back soon."

"There's no time to wait. I must go. I will meet her on the way." He grabbed his mother into a smothering hug. "I'll love you forever, Maman. Say goodbye to Papa and also to the children." He gestured to the loft where the children had gone to play. "I can't bear to tell them I won't be going with them." He paused at the door. "Tell Papa I'm doing this for him. There will be Héberts in L'Acadie again one day, I promise you."

"*Bonne chance*," Sarah said to François as he prepared to leave. The words sounded hollow to her. There was so much she wanted to tell Anne, but the time had run out and she had missed her opportunity. "Tell Anne I will never forget her. She will always be my Acadian sister."

"We are thankful for all you have done. Anne will miss you greatly."

Sarah stood at the door as François bolted toward the forest. Finally, she went back to the table where the two mothers comforted each other, tears streaming down their faces. Sarah's whole body trembled. It wasn't supposed to be like this. She had planned to say goodbye to Anne, to wish her luck, to tell her how much her friendship had meant. But it was too late. Anne was gone forever, and Sarah realized she would never know if Anne and François made it to safety.

That night, after Madame Hébert settled her brood in the loft, Sarah bedded down on the floor of the main room in front of the fireplace. It wasn't as cozy as the loft, but Sarah didn't expect to sleep much anyway. She had been so consumed with the dire situation here she hadn't given much thought to her own mother or grandparents. But now she thought about how she would feel if she knew she would never see any of her family again. It was a difficult choice Anne and François had been forced to make. But knowing a little about the life that awaited the Acadians in the colonies, Sarah was convinced they had made the right choice.

Chapter 20

I t was still dark out when a creaking hinge woke Sarah.
She opened her eyes and saw Luke peeking in the door.
Thank goodness he had made it back safely. She motioned
to him not to say anything, gathered the quilt around her,
and pulled on her moccasins. She gestured to the door. She
had no idea what time it was, but everyone was asleep and
she didn't want to wake them.

Luke and Sarah slipped out the door and made their way
quickly to the barn where they could talk. The rain had
stopped now. Sarah knew there would be no more delays to
prevent Winslow and his men from filling the boats with
Acadian families.

"Are François and Anne all right?" Sarah asked. The barn

wasn't exactly leak-proof, but she managed to find a dry spot beside the Hébert cart.

"Yeah, I think they're going to be OK," Luke said. "François stayed for a couple of hours in the hideout to be sure he hadn't been followed, then he joined Anne at the camp. Some of the other men will camp out there longer, but François and Anne are travelling tonight with the Mi'kmaq. The chief of the band decided it would be best to move on quickly, so I helped take down the wigwams of the remaining families. It's a pretty slick system they have. I was amazed at how quickly the camp could be dismantled."

"I'm glad that they've already left. The sooner, the better, I think. Did you see any soldiers on your way back?"

"No. It's quiet out there right now, but I'm sure there will be a search in the morning for the escaped men."

"What do you think Winslow will do when he finds out?" Sarah asked.

"According to what I read, I think he will make threats to the families, like telling them he'll burn all their belongings. He'll want their help to talk the men into returning."

"He won't really follow through, though, will he? What would be the point?"

"He'll put a scare into them, I'm sure, but I think you're right. He just wants to be out of here. And, despite everything, I think he is a decent guy."

"I do too. I read that he despised the awful task he was given."

"So, are we set to go? We should put on our real clothes under these other ones."

"Good idea. I almost forgot that I have other clothes. I want to help Maman LeBlanc before we leave, though," Sarah added. "Look at this cart. Maman LeBlanc's will be the same. The two women will never be able to manage all the children and the carts."

"You're not going down to the beach, are you? What's to stop the soldiers from shoving you onto a longboat that's headed for a transport ship?"

"I can't just go off and leave them — especially Maman LeBlanc. She's been like a mother to me."

"Maybe you could go with them most of the way, and then right before they get to the beach you could double back. I'll wait for you here in the barn, and then we could make a break for the dyke."

Sarah thought for a moment about this idea. "I'd still feel like a bit of a coward — sneaking off without even seeing if they find Papa LeBlanc and everything."

"A coward? Sarah, we're talking life and death here. And besides, short of travelling with them, you're never going to know if they're OK."

Sarah sighed. "I know you're right. But there *must* be some way . . ." Her voice trailed off as she tried to remember any useful detail from all the research she had done. "We aren't really Acadians," Sarah said, thinking out loud. "What if we could prove that we aren't Acadians?"

"Like saying that we're from the twenty-first century?" Luke retorted. "That ought to work well."

Sarah ignored the sarcasm. "What if we were someone important? Someone from Halifax."

"OK. So even if we did come up with some important identity, what would we be doing on the beach during the deportation of the Acadians?"

"Journalists! That's it! Do you remember me telling you about the *Halifax Gazette* being in operation in 1755?"

"Vaguely."

"I could be Elizabeth Bushell, covering the deportation story."

"I don't know." Luke rubbed his eyes. He looked totally exhausted. "What if they don't buy it?"

"I speak perfect English. Why wouldn't they believe me?"

"I'm not sure how rational the soldiers intend on being during this whole process, but I wouldn't count on it."

"All right, forget the journalist angle. I'll go with Maman LeBlanc to the beach, and then I'll leave right away, while other families are still making their way to the beach. There's bound to be a lot of confusion before they finish filling the ships. They won't have time to follow up on a stray Acadian girl wandering about. I'll meet you here in the barn, as you suggested, and then we'll head to the dyke."

"I think that's a better plan."

"Here," Sarah handed Luke the quilt she had wrapped around her. "Take this. You might as well get a bit of sleep while I help Maman LeBlanc pack the cart. I'm not sure when we'll get the word to start moving to the beach, but we need to be ready." Luke helped her manoeuvre the empty cart out the barn door.

Sarah was on her way to the house when soldiers rode up the path to the house. She crouched behind the cart.

"Take what you can carry and meet down at the shore! Orders from Colonel Winslow," the soldiers bellowed, barely even stopping in front of the door. "Immediately!" With that they rode away.

Sarah set the cart down by the front stoop and went inside. "I heard the soldiers," Sarah said softly to Maman LeBlanc. "I'll help you load the cart."

Maman simply nodded. Jean-Paul and Jeanne both clung to her skirts asking why they had to leave their house. "I don't know, my little ones," Maman answered. "I don't know. But you will be good, yes? And don't talk to the soldiers."

Sarah quickly gathered some things into sacks that the children could carry, while Maman began loading the things she had set aside. Madame Hébert got the children dressed in warm clothes and gave them their sacks to carry. Soon Maman's cart overflowed with clothes, blankets and every precious baking utensil, dish and tool, along with all the dried food and tins of herbs she had prepared.

Sarah ran to the barn to tell Luke that they were leaving. Several animals wandered around outside the barn. What would become of them? Sarah wondered. Were the soldiers going to feed them and look after them? She hoped so.

✿

Slowly, Sarah and the two families made their way to the shores of Minas Basin with hundreds of other women and children. Many of the women looked old, exhaustion etched into the lines of their tear-streaked faces. Some balanced babies on their hips, pushing their carts, while others had small children clutching their skirts, making progress almost impossible. They passed one family whose cart had overturned, spreading all their belongings across the mucky dirt road where others trampled over them in their own panicked efforts. Sarah stopped to help them pick up their things, but a soldier poked her ribs with his musket and told her to keep moving. She glared at him as she wiped the mud off her hands onto her apron.

The scene at the basin proved to be even more horrific as hysterical women searched for loved ones. Grandparents sat atop the meagre belongings of their families, embarrassed and humiliated. Some people had even tried to bring their chickens with them. Stray dogs barked and roamed through the mob looking for the families that had abandoned them.

They found a sheltered grassy slope near the water's edge and set down their carts.

"I have to go now." Sarah's voice trembled but she bit her lip, determined not to cry.

"Where will you go, my golden-haired angel?" Maman stroked the strands of hair that escaped Sarah's kerchief.

"It's time for me to go home," Sarah said gently.

Maman didn't ask anything further.

"I will miss you all." Sarah could barely get the words out. She hugged the children tightly. It was very hard to let them go.

As Sarah disappeared up the grassy slope there was a steady stream of women and children still arriving at the beach. Shouts from soldiers caught her attention and she looked up. Soldiers carrying muskets marched with a group of Acadian men along the beach. It must be the men from the church, Sarah thought. She knew she should hurry, but she had to be sure Papa LeBlanc found his family. The news spread like wild-fire that the men were now on the beach and a huge commotion broke out. Women left their belongings to find their husbands and sons, and the soldiers appeared to be totally unprepared for the mob scene that surrounded them. Sarah felt like joining the fray to find Papa LeBlanc and lead him to where his wife and children were, but she held back. With the flurry of activity she had lost sight of Maman and the children. Maybe they, too, were making their way along the beach to find Papa and Mathieu. And then the crowd shifted again, and she saw them. Thankfully, Papa had found them. She couldn't see their faces, but she knew the reunion was a happy one. Papa LeBlanc hoisted Jeanne high in the air and Maman looked like she was squeezing the stuffing out of Mathieu. Sarah swallowed hard and said a little prayer that their long journey would be a safe one. They were strong people. They would find a way to survive in the new place.

Sarah slowly made her way along the embankment, then she turned back for one more glimpse of her special Acadian family, the scene before her as surreal as some history movie. "You will always be in my heart," she uttered softly. "I wish it could have been different."

As she turned to leave, Sarah bumped smack into a red coat with shiny gold buttons.

"Wrong way," the soldier said, gesturing toward the beach.

In the split second it took Sarah to decide whether or not to run, he jabbed his musket into her. "This way," he said. "I am going to personally see to it that you are accommodated on the next long boat leaving for the ships. We don't need you people wandering around here endlessly."

"I'm Elizabeth Bushell from the *Halifax Gazette*," she blurted. It was the first thing that came to her mind.

The soldier stopped. "You're English?"

"I am. And unless you wish the story to depict the rudeness of the troops brought up from Boston, I suggest you take that gun off me."

"A woman of the press? Sounds like rubbish to me."

Sarah turned slowly. The soldier was not much taller than her and not much older either, she suspected.

"Why would a young Englishwoman be dressed as a French peasant, especially when the French Neutrals are being shipped off?" His eyes narrowed as he scrutinized her suspiciously. "And ye speak with a strange accent," he added.

"I didn't want to stand out . . ." Sarah began.

"Let her go. She isn't Acadian."

The sound of yet another English speaker startled the soldier so that he turned and momentarily moved his musket away from Sarah. She reached down, grabbed a handful of rocky sand and flung it with all her might into the soldier's face.

The soldier swore profusely as he attempted to rub his eyes.

"Run!" Sarah yelled at Luke as she grasped his hand.

"Through the crowd ahead," Luke said, steering them towards a family with small children and several animals. Sarah understood immediately what Luke was doing. The soldier would be less likely to fire into a crowd, and it would be harder to follow them. As they scrambled along the grassy bank and away from the beach Sarah glanced behind her in time to see the soldier stumble into a crate of chickens. The splinters and feathers flying everywhere would have been funny in a different situation. As it was, Sarah wasn't sure how much the chickens would slow down an already irate soldier.

Once they were away from the beach it was easier to run. Sarah's side was hurting but she willed herself to keep going. She wasn't sure what the punishment would be for attacking a soldier, but she didn't intend to find out. They had to reach the dyke.

They passed several women straggling toward the beach,

but fortunately they didn't encounter any soldiers. It felt as though they had been running for an eternity when Sarah saw the dyke stretching across the horizon in front of them. That gave her the burst of adrenaline she needed for the final push. She urged her rubbery legs to carry her to the top of the dyke. Only then did Sarah look back toward the beach. "I guess he decided we weren't worth the effort," she said, breathing hard from the run.

"Yeah. Let's not wait around to find out."

Sarah reached into the woven bag for the precious quill box. Before she took the lid off, she linked her arm through Luke's and gazed lovingly over the verdant valley. This time she would not be back.

At that moment, shouts rose up in the distance and orange flames shot into the grey skies. The soldiers were burning the cottages already. Before nightfall, Grand-Pré would be reduced to a pile of ashes. Sarah couldn't watch any longer. She squeezed her eyes closed and lifted the lid of the quill box.

Chapter 21

Sarah opened her eyes. Everything was still. Only a faint breeze rippled through the dry grass. The afternoon sun had been replaced with the golden glow of the moon.

"We made it, Sarah. We're home."

Sarah smiled weakly. She knew she should feel relieved. The quill box hadn't let them down. But she didn't feel relieved — she felt sick. Unable to put any of the raging emotions she felt into words, she simply took Luke's hand as they made their way to Maggie's.

Maggie's office door was closed so they were able to make it up the stairs unnoticed. Exhaustion sapped all of Sarah's strength but she knew she'd never be able to sleep. Her mind reeled from the events of the past couple of days, and she needed time to sort through everything that had happened. Maybe a hot bath would relieve her aching muscles. Nothing would ease her aching heart.

Within a few minutes, Sarah was soaking in the luxurious bubbles, her legs outstretched in Maggie's deep claw-foot tub. The steamy water worked wonders with her sore muscles. How many nights in the past month had she dreamed of soaking in a hot tub? But it did little to wash away the horror of recent events. She wanted to believe that it was all a ghastly nightmare — that none of it really happened. But it had happened and she knew the vivid images of those final days, final hours, would be with her forever. Sarah pulled the plug and watched until the last of the bubbles slid down the drain. How could she go back to her cozy, comfortable life? She wrapped herself tightly in her fuzzy robe, as if that could somehow protect her from the hurt, then she trod wearily down the stairs. Perhaps tea would help. Maman LeBlanc thought tea could cure anything.

Sarah made some tea and sank into the comfy chair by the fireplace. She wondered if Luke had been able to fall asleep.

"What's troubling you, dear?"

Sarah started. She hadn't even noticed Maggie sitting there.

"I thought it was a fine party."

"Party?" Sarah tried to pull her thoughts together. Her grandfather's party. That seemed like years ago now.

"Your grandfather loved his painting," Maggie continued. "Did you see his face? I've never seen him so happy."

Sarah nodded. It was good to hear Maggie's calm, soothing voice. "Yes, he did like it, I think." It seemed suddenly insignificant, petty even.

"You've a furrow in your forehead that's as deep as the Grand Canyon, girl. Want to talk about it?" Maggie paused as though deciding what to say next. "It's not about the party is it, love?"

"No," Sarah murmured. "It's not about the party." She drew in a deep breath trying to summon strength to continue. "I was thinking about friends of mine. They faced a huge crisis." Maggie listened intently. "I tried to help them," Sarah continued, "but in the end there was so little I could do." Sarah stared into space as tears leaked from the corners of her eyes. "It just wasn't enough." Her mind filled with pictures of her days in L'Acadie. The sweet bubbly Anne who always stood up for her and always trusted her. She had truly been a wonderful friend, practically a sister. But she couldn't free her mind of the images of Anne setting off alone in the pouring rain, never to see her family again and Maman huddled below the grassy bank with the children, leaving their cozy cottage and their beloved L'Acadie forever. Tears flowed freely now. There was no holding back.

Maggie handed her some tissues. "Tears are very cleansing, I find. Nothing better for the soul than a good hard cry sometimes."

Sarah couldn't have stopped the flood even if she tried. It

was as though she had spent the past few weeks damming up the emotion and now the dam had broken. Utterly drained, she closed her eyes and fell asleep in a ball on the cosy chair. She felt a warm blanket being tucked around her and heard Maggie pad softly up the stairs. She was too exhausted even to mumble a thank you or a good night.

But the world of sleep was not a tranquil one. There were loud voices shouting at her. Anne needed her to find François, and Jeanne was begging her to pick blueberries. Maman's voice cried for Sarah to rescue Papa from the church. Just then a soldier grabbed her and forced her into a boat.

"NO! I'm not Acadian!" Sarah shouted at them. "I have to go home!"

"Sarah, wake up." Luke touched her arm lightly and then grasped her hand. "It's all right," his gentle voice assured her. "We're home."

Sarah uncurled her legs and sat up in the chair where she had fallen asleep. The dream had been so vivid, so horrifyingly real. "Did I wake you?"

"No. I came downstairs to talk to you but you were asleep so I thought I'd just hang out here for a while. You did kind of scare me, though." He grinned. "I'll make us some toast and hot chocolate. I don't think either of us will sleep much tonight."

Luke whistled while he heated up the milk and made the toast. Sarah appreciated his effort at some kind of normalcy. She knew this had been hard on him too. They stared into the fire, comforted by the warm cocoa and each other's presence. Words could be hopelessly inadequate at times.

Finally Luke broke the silence. "You did what you could, Sarah. We both did."

Sarah felt the warm cocoa slide down her throat as she mulled over all the risks they both had taken. They hadn't abandoned their friends in time of need.

"I hope they made it." Sarah's voice was no more than a whisper.

"I do too."

Chapter 22

Sarah felt a warm glow as she sat at her grandmother's dining room table surrounded by friendly faces that had been strangers only a couple of months ago. It was sweet of her grandparents to invite Maggie and Luke for her farewell dinner. She would miss them a lot.

"I would like to propose a toast," her jovial grandfather began as soon as everyone was seated, "to our artist extraordinaire and the best granddaughter anyone could ever hope for, Miss Sarah White." He raised his crystal wine glass. "May life bring as much happiness to you, as you have brought to us. Tomorrow you will leave our home, but you will never leave our hearts."

Sarah blushed at the lavish praise from her grandfather.

"This has been a summer I'll never forget." She glanced at Luke. "I couldn't ask for better friends and family than the ones I've gotten to know this summer. I'm really going to miss you all."

Only Luke, with his subtle smile, understood that the friends extended beyond the ones presently gathered at the table.

Her grandmother beamed with pride. "You were a delight to have around, dear. I must say I have never known a teenager to be so interested in the local history."

"Speaking of local history," Maggie interjected between bites of baked potato. "I have some pretty exciting news. I've been digging in that trunk that this pair unearthed in my attic. You'll never in a million years guess what I found." She paused to cut up her slice of roast beef. "A folded piece of yellowed paper fell out of one of the old books in there. It was the Hébert family tree — goes back almost to the expulsion of the Acadian people. Can you beat that?" Maggie shook her head in amazement. "It ended at my grandparents. I was some surprised I'll tell you. I thought all that stuff was George's old navy books and such, but I guess some of the stuff from my folks' house got dumped in there when my mother passed away. Anyways, I'm going to get it framed and put it up in my sitting room."

"Have you seen it, Luke?" Sarah couldn't keep the excitement out of her voice.

"Yeah, I did, but as Maggie says it starts after the deportation." Luke knew exactly what Sarah was getting at.

"You do beat all," Reta White commented. "You even get excited about someone else's history."

"It's just that it's remarkable to have a family tree that goes back so far," Sarah commented. "I don't even know who my father is." An awkward silence fell over the group and Sarah wished she could take back that last comment. She sounded like such a baby.

"I know what Sarah means," Luke said. "There aren't many people who are handed a family tree that goes back so far. People spend years on the Internet and in archives to get that kind of information. In fact," he looked meaningfully at Sarah, "I think we should try to fill in the gaps all the way back to the deportation."

Pete White cleared his throat. "We have a little surprise of our own." He coughed nervously. "Reta and I have talked about it and we've decided that this would be the perfect time."

"Perfect time for what?" Sarah asked.

Her grandfather rose slowly out of his chair and hobbled down the hallway on one crutch.

"This is quite a day for surprises," Maggie commented.

"I'll say," Luke agreed.

Sarah's curiosity heightened when Pete White returned carrying a little worn velvet bag.

"Our family has a special keepsake as well." He spoke directly to Sarah. "We were saving this until you turned eighteen, but we've decided that now would be a better time.

Not that we're trying to compete with Maggie's family tree, but since you're so interested in the Acadians, we thought, why wait?"

"What is it, Grandpa? Don't keep me in such suspense."

He pulled out a little wooden cross on a thin leather lace. Sarah gasped. It couldn't possibly be. She took the cross and carefully turned it over. There etched inside a heart were the worn initials *A.H.* "I can't believe it," she murmured. "How did you get this?" She held the cross tightly in her hand. For a moment she could hardly breathe. Could this really be Anne's special cross?

Sarah's grandparents exchanged puzzled glances. "We didn't expect you to go into shock over this. You haven't even heard the story yet."

"I'm sorry," Sarah said thinking fast. "I know you're going to think this is crazy, but I had a dream about an Acadian girl and she was wearing a cross that looked just like this. It kind of caught me off guard, I guess."

"Well, that's the darnedest thing I ever heard." Her grandfather shook his head in disbelief. "Let me tell you the story. Back in 1755, several of the families that were deported from Grand-Pré ended up on a ship called the *Elizabeth* that was bound for Maryland. Conditions were horrible. The ship was overcrowded and they ran out of supplies. A lot of people died before they even got to their destination. When the surviving Acadians arrived in Maryland, they were met by a community who wasn't really expecting them.

Many Acadians were treated harshly and unfairly although it wasn't as bad there as it was in some of the colonies. Eventually it became obvious that if the next generation was to have any chance at all they would have to learn English, which of course was the intent of the British government all along. Anyways, many of the LeBlancs did just that. They learned English and changed their name to White."

"So, we're Acadian?" Sarah struggled to take all of this in.

"Indeed we are," Grandpa said proudly. "Twenty-seven years after the deportation some of the families left for Nova Scotia as United Empire Loyalists. The Whites were among them."

"Amazing," Luke mumbled.

Her grandfather continued, "This cross was passed down through the generations as a reminder of what the Acadians suffered at the hands of the English. Regardless of what they called themselves or what language they spoke, deep down they would always be Acadian."

"But the initials on the back are *A.H.*," Sarah pointed out. She was sure this was Anne's cross but what was the connection to the White family?

Pete White smiled. "You're quite the detective. There's more to the story. The initials stood for Anne Hébert, but her maiden name was LeBlanc. Apparently Anne and her betrothed husband, François Hébert, managed to escape into the forest and travel with the Mi'kmaq. And years later, a Mi'kmaq friend told Anne of a story she had recently heard about a man who claimed that when he was a young boy, shortly before his family had been deported, he had been saved from drowning by a golden-haired angel."

Sarah felt the tears ready to burst into a flood and fled to the bathroom. She patted her face with a cold cloth and took several deep breaths. That man must have been Jean-Paul. The family had made it — and they had lived to tell stories to their children and grandchildren. She went back to the dining room as calmly as possible. She had to hear the rest of the story.

"Are you feeling sick, Sarah?" her grandmother asked when she returned.

"No, I'm fine. I felt like I couldn't breathe for a minute, but I'm fine now." She faced her grandfather. "Please finish the story."

"Well, it seems like Anne had the same reaction to the story. Her youngest brother had been saved from drowning by a young blond woman who wasn't from the area. She immediately found out where he was living and made the trip to visit him in Grand-Pré. Sure as anything, it was her baby brother, now a full grown man with a family of his own. He had changed his name to John White. That probably bothered Anne some. Apparently Jean-Paul offered to build her a home on his land — François was no longer living. But Anne and François had made their home along the north shore of what is now New Brunswick, and she had no desire to return to Grand-Pré. Before she left, she gave the cross to Jean-Paul's son as a reminder of his Acadian roots. Ever since then it's been passed down to the oldest grand-child.

Sarah wrinkled her forehead, confused. "Acadians were never given back their farm lands."

Her grandfather chuckled. "That's the irony of it all. Anne's brother, Jean-Paul, married into an English family who was granted a tract of land in Grand-Pré, so almost three decades after being deported, he was able to come home. He paused for a moment, looking thoughtful. "Since you are the only grandchild, the responsibility of carrying on the tradition falls to you. There was a time when I worried about that, but when you gave me your beautiful Acadian painting, it was like a sign. I knew the cross had found its home."

"This is the most treasured gift anyone has ever given me." Sarah looked incredulously at the cross, then embraced both of her grandparents. "Do you mind if Luke and I go out for a walk? We have some things to talk over before I leave."

Maggie and her grandparents exchanged knowing glances.

"Go ahead dear," Reta answered, making no attempt to hide her smug smile.

"Can you believe it?" Sarah blurted the moment they were out the door. "Anne survived and Jean-Paul survived and we are actually related." Sarah thought back to her first day in L'Acadie when she saved Jean-Paul's life. "It's all so overwhelming."

"I'll say," Luke agreed. "In some ways, I'm glad it's over. I'm exhausted. In some ways I wish it would never end." He took her hand in his.

"I know what you mean." They walked a few moments in silence both enveloped in their own thoughts about the events of the summer.

"So, what's next, Sarah?"

"Next, I go back to Toronto and try to live a normal life, I guess."

"Would you consider staying here and going to school?" Luke asked tentatively.

"I never really thought of that as an option."

"You could, you know. Your grandparents would be thrilled to have you move in with them for a year. You could go to school here and we could hang out still."

"That would be great . . ."

"But? I distinctly hear a 'but' at the end of that sentence."

Sarah smiled. He knew her so well. "*But* I need to go home." Sarah stared off into the distance. "I'm not the same person I was at the start of the summer."

"No kidding!"

Sarah punched him playfully on the arm. "Seriously, if I stayed here, I'd feel like I was running away from the problems with my mother. I think I need to be more honest with her and tell her how I feel. I haven't really given her a chance."

"I didn't think you'd stay, but it was worth a shot. You can't blame a guy for trying."

Sarah knew that going back to Toronto was the right thing to do. She also knew that she couldn't say good-bye to the one person who had shared all her joys, fears and heartbreak during this unforgettable summer. "Don't worry, I won't be able to stay away for long." Sarah linked her arm through Luke's and looked wistfully toward Minas Basin. "This is my home."

ABOUT THE AUTHOR

Lois Donovan was born in Montreal, but grew up primarily in Riverview, New Brunswick, prior to attending Acadia University in Nova Scotia. After completing her education degree in Edmonton, Lois taught there for three years before making Calgary home. Through her experience of living in various provinces in Canada, Lois developed a keen interest in writing stories for children and young adults based on Canadian history. Her love of the beautiful Annapolis Valley sparked an interest in retelling the tragic tale of the Acadian people, which resulted in her first novel, *Winds of L'Acadie*.

In addition to writing, Lois enjoys the unique perspective of seeing life through the eyes of her university-aged son, and her toddler daughter. Lois is currently teaching and writing in Calgary where she lives with her husband and daughter.

Lois enjoys hearing from her readers. She can be reached by email at writestuff@loisdonovan.com. Her website can be found at www.loisdonovan.com.

Marquis Book Printing Inc.

Québec, Canada
2011